Dorothy Eden
DEATH IS A RED ROSE

When Cressida Lucy Barclay
decides to take the vacant flat in
the large decaying London
house, she knows that the terms
of her tenancy are odd, the
other occupants distinctly
unusual, and the landlady the
strangest of all. With her parrot,
her tarnished finery and her
passion for camels, Arabia
Bolton is truly flamboyant. She
is also unpredictable, especially
in her obsession with the
memory of her long-dead
daughter.

Cressida decides to stay. But
the more she delves into the
past, the more she senses a net
closing around her, a net whose
strands are closely interwoven
with the mystery of a dead girl
also called Cressida Lucy and
with a room where the scent of
red roses hangs heavy in the air.

DEATH IS A RED ROSE

When Cressida Lucy Barclay decides to take the vacant flat in the large decaying London house, she knows that the terms of her tenancy are odd, the other occupants distinctly unusual, and the landlady the strangest of all. With her parrot, her tarnished finery and her passion for camels, Arabia Bolton is truly flamboyant. She is also unpredictable, especially in her obsession with the memory of her long-dead daughter.

Cressida decides to stay. But the more she delves into the past, the more she senses a net closing around her, a net whose strands are closely interwoven with the mystery of a dead girl also called Cressida Lucy and with a room where the scent of red roses hangs heavy in the air.

DEATH IS A RED ROSE

Dorothy Eden

LARGE
PRINT

SCARLET
DAGGER
·CRIME·

**CHIVERS PRESS
BATH**

First published 1956
by
Macdonald & Co (Publishers) Ltd
This Large Print edition 1993 by Chivers Press
published by arrangement with
the author's estate

ISBN 0 7451 6444 7

British Library Cataloguing in Publication Data available

Photoset, printed and bound in Great Britain by
Redwood Books, Trowbridge, Wiltshire

FOREWORD

Dorothy Eden was brought up on a farm in Canterbury, New Zealand, in a large family. She had always longed to write and, having had some success with short stories, was encouraged to leave New Zealand when the war was over to come to England, bravely setting out to earn her living as a writer. She had sent a manuscript ahead of her to start her on her way: it launched her into twenty years of writing suspense fiction.

From the outset, she attracted a faithful reading public. These first books developed from her short stories; they were early examples of what came to be known as 'gothic' romances. But the romantic suspense story, with an intriguing mystery, has a long history, going back at least as far as *Jane Eyre*. In this category of book *Death Is a Red Rose*, first published in 1956, holds a well-deserved place.

An essential ingredient in these stories is an engaging heroine, who must be partnered by a strong hero. Good looks are not vital to either party, but they must have style. Jeremy Winter in *Death Is a Red Rose* has shaggy black hair and a bony jaw, but he is an artist and has charisma and force. Mr Rochester, the beloved of Jane Eyre, was downright ugly, but he had tremendous sex appeal, some wit, and a secret. The secret is another vital element in a 'gothic' hero, and Dorothy Eden excelled in producing such men. Tim Royle in *The Voice of the Dolls* is an excellent example. He appears first in a subordinate position, as a gardener, but we soon guess he is much more. They are neither smooth men, nor bores. And while not necessarily rich, they are succeeders. And quite rightly, because they are matched with girls of spirit.

The heroine is the centre of the story. She provides the action; she bears the weight of the mystery, and all the danger. It is she who will resolve the puzzle at the heart of the story, and it is her life that will be rewarded with a happy ending. Cressida Barclay, at the end of *Death Is a Red Rose*, knows that in Jeremy she has found someone with whom to share all the jokes of life. Not a bad recipe for living happily ever after!

Such a heroine never bears the burden of great beauty, but will always have a kind of bonny good looks. She is also plucky and intelligent, although she may have a secret sorrow. Harriet Lacey in *Listen to Danger* is a young widow; Sarah in *The Voice of the Dolls* has just lost her father.

In the cast of characters assembled by Dorothy Eden in her suspense novels, I have not mentioned one of the most important: the child. Children are frequently at the heart of the story, as in *Listen to Danger* or *The Voice of the Dolls*. Was it just a foible of Dorothy Eden, or is it crucial to the romantic suspense thriller? Remember that in *Jane Eyre* there is a child, centre stage. It might be thought that the child is just a device to get the heroine into the company of characters, alien to her, around whom the story is spun. But in Dorothy Eden's case the children are important in themselves. She was sympathetic to the child, especially to the lonely unhappy child like Jennie in *The Voice of the Dolls*. Her children are individuals, treated with dignity, humour and respect: they are among her strengths. It is worth noting, however, that Dawson Stanhope, the child in *Death Is a Red Rose*, is not an attractive character, yet the mother-child relationship is central to the plot.

By the time of her death in 1982, Dorothy Eden's sales were considerable; she attracted a huge audience worldwide eager to read her books. She was able to command this following because, quite simply, she was a splendid storyteller.

GWENDOLINE BUTLER

CHAPTER ONE

For perhaps the first time in seventy-five years Arabia Bolton found life dull beyond endurance. A few days ago the rather amusing sculptor who disagreed violently with everything she said, but who, for that very reason, entertained her (she dearly loved a quarrel), had vacated the ground-floor flat, and she found she missed his visits to her untidy overflowing rooms upstairs more than she would have believed.

There was no one else in the house whom she cared to make a friend. Perhaps the tall young man, Jeremy Winter, in the basement. He had a twinkling eye and a nice wit. But he was too polite. She liked a broad, even a risqué style. Anyway, he was too young to want to spend time with an old lady absorbed in the past.

The past ... Arabia glanced briefly round the large room that would have been museum-like, had any museum that rich haphazard untidiness. Rather, it was like an untended garden, heavy-headed dahlias and over-blown roses mingling with the delicate plants that scarcely showed their heads. There was that miniature of Lucy, incredibly innocent and fair, completely overshadowed by the portrait of herself at the age of sixty with the parrot on her shoulder. There were the trophies she had picked up in her journeys, an Arab's headdress, camel bells, spears and gourds rubbing shoulders with Victorian ornaments. She loved masses of cushions in bright colours, and they flowed over the couches and on

1

to the floor. The lampshades were long-tasselled and in similar gaudy colours. The gilt parrots' cages were made in the shape of Bedouin tents. One of them contained the active and vociferous Ahmed, the other his predecessor who was now no more than a light handful of stuffed rose and pearl-grey feathers. Persian rugs (she remembered with vivid nostalgia the hot-smelling, dusty Baghdad bazaars) completely covered a very fine parquet floor. If ever Jeremy Winter's yellow cat found his way up here he had a fine time springing and slipping on the rugs, while Ahmed the parrot went wild with excitement and screeched deafeningly, and as likely as not one of the Dresden or Meissen figures was knocked over and broken.

Everything in the room, Arabia was wont to say, told a story. But stories required listeners, and now she had none. What was the use of a colourful and fantastic past if there was no one to whom to recount it? And just anybody would not do. Arabia was critical as to her audience. It had to be both intelligent and appreciative, and preferably argumentative, although she would be willing for admiration and affection to take the place of the argumentativeness. It would be nice to be loved and admired in one's declining years. If Lucy...

Arabia sighed. No use to go over that. Things were as they were, and she was a lonely old woman in a house of strangers, and suddenly life was dull.

She had begun to let rooms several years ago. It was absurd for one old woman and a couple of servants to live alone in such a large house.

2

Besides, servants were hard to keep. If it were not that the house was too big, it was Ahmed screeching at them, or Arabia, with a whim to wear the Arab headdress, frightening them out of their wits, silly creatures.

So she had had the brilliant idea of taking in lodgers, thus killing three birds with one stone—making a little extra money which she enjoyed but did not need, having company, and making the arrangement that one of the lodgers should act as a servant.

The scheme had worked beautifully. She had had a series of gay and interesting people, sometimes a little eccentric like herself (there had been the artist who had painted his walls with slightly Bacchanalian murals which had had to be hurriedly painted over on his departure). The middle-aged and poverty-stricken daughter of a sea captain, Gloriana Becker, who had taken the ballroom, moving her meagre possessions into the enormous room so that her modest bedstead looked like a lonely tent in the desert, had been with Arabia faithfully for five years and filled the rôle of a maid excellently. She was willing to cook and do housework for the rent of her room. She was too poor for false pride. The care of the captain, a peppery and domineering invalid, had taken both her youth and all the money she might have expected to inherit. Now she was growing as peppery as her father had been, and Arabia naughtily encouraged her into displays of temper, simply to relieve the boredom.

But one desiccated spinster with a sharp temper was not enough to make life interesting. All at once, in her seventy-sixth year, Arabia discovered that she had let her rooms unwisely, allowing her sympathy to run away with her sense, and there was no one, except possibly Jeremy Winter, to whom she could talk. She thought she might try out the story of the sheik and the ten camels on him and see how he reacted. It was an infallible test. Then suddenly she found that she was tired and wasn't sure that she wanted to tell that story any more. Life was empty, squeezed dry. There was no more relish to it. She was a lonely and unloved old woman. In her reckless impetuous life she had given so much, and yet she had come to this. It wasn't fair. Even that wretched little Mrs. Stanhope on the first floor, who could speak only in an unintelligible whisper, had a son to love her. No very bright specimen, Dawson, weak-eyed and with a sly look to him, but with devotion and love to give his mother.

Then there was the violinist, Vincent Moretti. He, with his quick, pale glance, had the look of having an endless fund of good stories to tell, but unexpectedly he had proved disappointing. He had little to say to Arabia and indeed was inclined to avoid her. He spent most of the day practising (with a taste for dirge-like music), and during his idle moments carried on a harmless and probably quite meaningless flirtation with the suddenly coy Miss Glory. This, Arabia found exasperating in the extreme, and extracted what meagre entertainment she could from it by making constant sly digs at Miss Glory on the subject of virtue.

Jeremy Winter in the basement had not been welcomed so much on account of his potential value as an amusing and diverting guest as because he was a broad-shouldered, strong young man and the basement had, in the past, proved a happy hunting ground for burglars. After two burglaries, in both of which Arabia had lost some of her extraordinary collection of ornate jewellery, she had decided that window bars were not enough. She must turn the basement into a flat and let it to an alert and courageous person. Her advertisement: 'Wanted a tenant willing to catch burglars', had produced a motley collection of applicants. Jeremy had been quite the best. He had smiled at her then with that lifting eyebrow and twinkle that promised so much, and had said that he would bring, also, his cat Mimosa who would catch mice.

Arabia had been delighted, and sure that behind his politeness there was a great deal to the young man. But at that time her quarrelsome friendship with the sculptor on the ground floor had been at its height and she was fully occupied. Now the sculptor had gone, and the ground-floor flat was empty, and she was dull, dull...

What amusing advertisement should she put in the evening papers this time? 'Ground-floor flat in mansion to let. Grand piano or lap dog not objected to.' Or 'Applicant must have a mind'. In the past she had had some diverting moments in wording advertisements and seeing what they produced. But suddenly she was so tired. Did she want a tenant with a mind? Did she want murals or dissertations on Cretan-age morals? Wouldn't a dull cabbage be preferable now that she was growing so old? Then she would have the house full of cabbages: Mrs. Stanhope and the tall skinny Dawson, Miss Glory with her sudden intolerable coyness, the elusive Vincent Moretti, Jeremy—no, his qualities had still to be tested...

Arabia looked round her cluttered room. Did she want any more uproarious evenings of telling tales about her old friend, the sheik, of dressing in her Turkish clothes and singing clever naughty songs to the accompaniment of the zither, of teasing Ahmed with the stuffed parrot until he nearly brought the plaster roses on the ceiling down with his hysterical screeching. No, all at once she wanted peace. And love. Particularly love. And who in all the world was there left to love her?

Men still liked her because, although she was old and now quite ugly, she still retained her majestic carriage, and the glamour she had always had was indestructible. But they no longer fell madly in love with her—thank heaven for that at least. Even the memory of that was now curiously wearying. And when she thought back the strange thing was that, for all the love she had enjoyed and for all the intoxicating satisfaction of the power she had over men, the thing that pleased her most was her remembered love for Lucy. It ran like a pure thread through those rich, overflowing days, like the perfume of primroses in a room full of spices. It was clean and delightful, it was like the thought of spring during a burning dry summer.

But now it was gone and she was so lonely. There was no way to bring back the spring.

Or was there? Arabia suddenly straightened herself among the crushed cushions. All at once she was erect, her old head held at its indomitable angle. She, Arabia Bolton, who had crooked her finger and the world had come to her, who all her life had got what she wanted, why could she not bring back the spring? Why indeed could she not?

Her old fingers trembling with excitement and impatience, she pulled out the drawers of her writing-desk and tumbled old letters and bills on to the floor. She found some of her expensive engraved notepaper, unused for a long time. She wrote in her thick black writing:

WANTED TO LET GROUND-FLOOR FLAT IN LARGE WEST END HOUSE. RENT NOMINAL FOR ATTRACTIVE GIRL WHOSE NAMES MUST BE CRESSIDA LUCY. APPLY IN PERSON.

Arabia breathed heavily, chuckling with excitement. What a brilliant idea, what a scintillating, brilliant idea. Who said she could not bring back the spring? She who had power to do so much, she would have power over the seasons, too.

Cressida ... Cressida Lucy ... Lucy...

Oh, Lucy, I loved you...

I hate you, I hate you...

That voice, suddenly ringing in her head, thin and vicious, was not there, really. It was in her imagination, as so much else had been. There, it had gone already; the blackness it had brought over her had gone, too. She was rejuvenated, full of life and excitement. It was springtime, and she was going to have another Lucy, young, innocent, new. Another Lucy to love her and to be loved...

CHAPTER TWO

Cressida opened her eyes and saw the young man. She promptly shut them again, partly because she was extraordinarily tired and partly because she wanted to think in a comfortably anonymous darkness. Her open eyes would betray her utter bewilderment. Until she knew where she was, how she had got there and who the strange young man was it was better to remain composed and apparently sane.

It might still be a dream, of course. She sometimes had very vivid dreams. Once she had even walked downstairs in her sleep, and when her mother had told Tom the next morning he, quite unperturbed, had said comfortably, 'I won't let her do that when we're married.'

Tom! Now she remembered. She had run away!

She sat up in a flurry, and the room swam. It was a large room with a raftered ceiling, rather sparsely furnished, but with a fire burning cheerfully. The largest piece of furniture was a desk. It was extremely littered with papers and on one side of it, on top of the scattered papers, sat a square and dour-looking yellow cat. Behind it was the young man. He had his head bent and seemed to be sketching.

He was real, Cressida told herself. He was not only not Tom, who until recently had dominated her life, but was not in the least like Tom, having rather shaggy black hair that hung forward over the brow, a bony jawline and a quick, nervous hand that moved absorbedly over the drawing-board.

What on earth would Tom say if he knew that she had been sleeping, however innocently, on the couch in the room of a complete stranger? Moreover, a stranger who was not, apparently, the least interested in her. Indeed, he was proceeding with his work as if she were either a piece of furniture or not there at all.

It was becoming increasingly evident to Cressida that she was there and that she had a very odd and rather unpleasant feeling in her stomach.

'Hi!' she said feebly.

The young man's head shot up, displaying a face as bony as the jawline, with slightly crooked black brows and very bright eyes.

'Well, there,' he said triumphantly, 'I knew you weren't dead. But just keep still a moment longer, will you.'

'Keep still!' Cressida repeated bewilderedly. But before her muzzy mind could work that out she was aware that she was clutching something in one hand. It was a crumpled piece of paper. She spread it out and read what was written on it in large scrawling writing. It said briefly, '*You're too late!*'

Then she began to remember. The little woman in the very large horn-rimmed glasses, whose fingers kept constantly and mysteriously pointing to her mouth, flitted across her vision like a noonday owl. She remembered the piece of paper being thrust in her hand, and her mingled relief and despair on reading the words. She had had a curiously urgent desire to get out of the house,

9

and yet where was she to go? The slippery marble steps had stretched before her, the big door with its shining dragon knocker had banged behind her. She had had the most curious feeling that the silent little woman in the too large glasses had enjoyed banging the door. And that had fitted in with her intuition that she should never have come into the house, anyway. But it was her tiredness that had made her slip.

She remembered seeing the shine of rain on the steps as she fell. And that was all.

Sudden urgent curiosity stirred life in her. She sat up straight and said imperiously,

'Do, for heaven's sake, stop what you are doing and tell me where I am.'

The yellow cat turned its head and gave her an incurious stare out of champagne-coloured eyes. The man, after a last deliberate movement of his pencil, looked up and smiled. One of his eyebrows lifted a little higher than the other. His face, when he smiled, went into deep lines, but his eyes had a twinkling brightness that seemed amused at her and her plight.

'At the moment you're on my couch,' he said. 'Ten minutes ago you were lying at the foot of the front steps. It was raining so I brought you in.'

'Thank you,' said Cressida inadequately. Now she was beginning to feel sundry aches and bruises. There seemed to be a painful lump on the back of her head. And her stomach felt definitely peculiar.

Presently, since the young man seemed to be staring at her so pointedly, she said diffidently, 'You didn't think a doctor was necessary?'

'You didn't seem to have broken anything. I

thought I'd wait a little while and see.' He got up and came over to her in a leisurely manner. He was very tall. 'Do you feel all right now?'

'Y-es,' Cressida said uncertainly. Her head was beginning to ache furiously, and her inside—'I think there's nothing that—'

'A small spot of brandy won't cure,' her host pronounced.

He disappeared at once, and Cressida heard glasses clinking in the adjoining room. The cat on the desk stood up, stretched himself, and, for all his bulk, gave a surprisingly light spring on to the couch. There he rubbed his head ingratiatingly against Cressida's hand, and began to purr.

Cressida permitted herself a tremulous smile. Here was someone who was friendly and unmysterious, anyway. The young man, coming back with a tray, smiled too, and said, 'Oh, that's splendid. Mimosa is extremely fussy about his friends. Now Arabia he won't allow to touch him.'

'Arabia? Who's he?'

'She. And you'll meet her presently if you stay. By the way, my name is Jeremy Winter.'

'Mine's Cressida Barclay.'

'Ah-h-h!' The exclamation was long-drawn-out and interested. 'So that explains it.'

'Explains what?'

'Why you came here. You're answering Arabia's crazy advertisement.'

'I was,' Cressida said confusedly. 'But I didn't really mean to. I got scared when I saw the house.'

'So you ran away and fell down the steps. Drink this, and tell me about it.'

11

Cressida looked at the brandy doubtfully. She didn't want to admit that if she drank it she would probably be sick. She knew now what was wrong with her stomach. She hadn't had anything to eat for quite a long time. Well, perhaps the brandy would do her good. At least it might make her feel more optimistic about the future.

Recklessly she took the glass from Jeremy Winter and swallowed the contents.

As was to be expected, the room swam again, but this time in rather a pleasant way. The firelight seemed to get mixed up with the brightness of Jeremy's eyes, and Mimosa's hair shone like sunlight. The sunlight and the firelight got into her stomach, too. They made it feel much better.

'I'm not going back,' she pronounced definitely.

'Good for you.'

'Tom would be so superior.'

'I suppose he would.'

Cressida blinked a little at the agreeable, unsurprised voice. She was beginning to feel very hazy indeed.

'Do you know Tom?'

'Not your Tom. But I know superior types. Are you married to him?'

'Oh no. We're only engaged. We're going to be married on the twelfth of June in 1957.'

'A long-term plan?' Jeremy put down his glass and picked up a pipe. 'Do you mind if I smoke?'

'Not in the least.' Pipe smoke, drifting fragrantly about, would add to this pleasant illusory sensation. 'Tom's very cautious,' she said.

'I gather he must be. How old is he?'

'Thirty, but I'm only twenty-two. He says

12

twenty-four is a better age for me to marry, and by that time, of course, he'll have paid for the house and furniture. We bought a bedroom suite the other day.'

'Did you?'

'Yes. In oak. Tom liked it.'

'And you?'

'I ran away,' Cressida said simply.

The room was a warm darkness studded here and there with light. She was dimly aware of one of Jeremy Winter's eyebrows lifting startlingly. She knew that he was laughing, but politely, inside himself. He wouldn't have laughed, she told herself grimly, if he had been her, and had seen that bedroom suite, heavy and dark and solid, seeming to weigh her down like a nightmare. She couldn't have explained to anybody, even to herself, the panic that had filled her, as if all the years ahead with Tom had pressed themselves into one suffocating moment.

'I love Tom,' she heard herself saying carefully, 'but it's a great pity that we have very dissimilar tastes. He really belongs to the Victorian period, he likes solid things that last forever, and I—'

'And you?'

'I could imagine all my babies being born in that awful great bed.' Cressida was very hot now, and a little light-headed. Mimosa curled up at her side, and settled down with a heavy purr of contentment. Jeremy, at the side of the couch, continued to laugh silently at her. She was in a dream, but at least it was not the dream that she was suffocating in that bed with Tom, with curtains drawn round it, as in the days of their great-grandparents, and a stuffy breathless darkness round them.

'I like pretty things,' she said. 'Fragile things. I know they don't last and they're extravagant, but who wants things to last forever? I like to buy flowers, and I like to give money to beggars. I like mending old china, and I like Dresden cupids. I can't cook and I'm not practical, but Tom doesn't mind that. He says I'll learn. This time he has to learn.'

'To cook?' Jeremy enquired politely.

'That he can't change me completely. A little, perhaps. But not completely. I'm not going back until then.'

'Tom, if you will allow me to say so, doesn't sound like the learning kind.'

Cressida smiled, suddenly tender about Tom and his stubbornness.

'Oh, yes, he will be. He loves me too much not to be.' She lay back, remembering Tom's kisses, trying in retrospect to invest them with all the tenderness and passion that she dreamed about. Suddenly her brief optimism and light-heartedness left her, and she wanted to cry because they had quarrelled so irretrievably, and now, although she was in this mess, her pride would not allow her to go back. It was a desperate situation.

'You aren't Tom's type,' she heard Jeremy Winter, who after all was a complete stranger and could have no way of knowing her or Tom, saying.

She struggled up.

'How can you possibly say that? You don't know either of us. After all we ought to know whether we are each other's type or not. We've

14

known each other for fifteen years.'

'The cradle to the grave?' That eyebrow was up at its irritating angle. 'Very well, you're made for each other, but in the meantime you're here in my room. What is Tom going to say about that?'

'Oh, he mustn't know!'

'Well, I don't propose to tell him. What about you?'

'I won't tell him either, and now I must go.'

She got safely to her feet in one quick movement. The yellow cat, at being disturbed, gave a grumble of protest. Cressida said, 'He's a very spoilt cat,' and sat shakily down. 'You've made me drunk,' she accused.

She was aware of his hand supporting her. The room spun crazily. She wanted to laugh and ended by crying. It was all so humiliating, and so different from what she had expected on her sanguine departure from home three days ago,

'You can't go yet, Cressida. I want to draw you. I've only just begun.' He stood over her, dominating her as Tom had done, but in a different way. She was tired of being dominated by men. She would do as she herself wished, for once. If her ridiculously weak legs would let her...

'You have just the face I have been looking for,' Jeremy Winter was saying thoughtfully. 'It's full of innocence, and yet it has sophistication and intelligence. An intriguing combination for a twenty-two-year-old. I'd like to rearrange your hair slightly. But we can do that at the next sitting.'

'The next sitting!' Cressida gasped.

'Tomorrow, if you like. When you're feeling

15

stronger.'

'But—but where am I to stay?'

'In Arabia's flat, of course. You're just the person she has been looking for. I know. My dear child, of course you couldn't sleep with Tom in that horrible bed.'

'W-what?'

'At least, not until he's learnt his lesson. And I shall have great pleasure in helping you to teach it to him, I promise you.' The dark, bright eyes twinkled, the eyebrow raised startlingly.

Cressida blinked. She said, 'Mim—Mimosa! What a ridiculous name for a cat.'

'Mimosa, I might tell you, is a celebrity. He appears in fifteen different advertisements and is the star in a comic strip. So he has cultivated a temperament. What would you like to eat?'

'To eat?'

'I rather think that is your immediate concern. When did you last eat?'

'Yesterday. I think it was yesterday. About six o'clock. I had a ham roll and a glass of milk. I didn't think I could get so hungry again so quickly. You see, the trouble was that when I left home I hadn't much money, and money goes awfully quickly in London. And I thought it would be much easier than it is to get a job. I'm sure I could sell things. I do know quite a lot about antiques. But nobody—' Her lip quivered. She tried to make the dark shadow of yesterday and the day before leave her mind. 'One thing, I was determined I wasn't going to let Tom know.'

'Naturally.'

'And then this morning I gave my last sixpence to a beggar. Well, he was blind, and I at least

16

could see.'

She looked at Jeremy defensively. She expected him to pity her illogical soft-heartedness, but he merely nodded, as if he had known she was going to confess to a thing like that.

'So then, although I'd come before to this house, and been frightened somehow and gone away—that advertisement was a little odd, after all, and one should be careful of those things—I knew I'd either have to come back here or send for Tom. And I decided at least I could see what happened here. No one was going to eat me, after all.'

'Not even Mimosa,' said Jeremy. 'Why were you frightened?'

'I don't know. I had the most curious feeling, as if I were someone else, and something awful would happen to me. I actually ran down the street. But today I came back, and the woman with the glasses said it was too late. And I slipped on the steps as I was leaving, and that's all I remember.'

'Do you like bacon and eggs?' Jeremy asked practically. 'Of course, I'll pay you for the sittings, and Arabia will be delighted—why, here she is now!'

And that was when Cressida had the odd feeling of the net, both fascinating and frightening, closing round her.

She heard the rich delighted voice behind her.

'Why, Jeremy, you naughty boy! You've got a woman here!'

'That serves you right for coming in without knocking. Mrs. Bolton, I want you to meet a friend of mine, Miss Cressida Barclay.'

'Cress—' The deep voice died away in astonished pleasure and disbelief. 'But I thought—you mean, she actually came!'

'She's here,' Jeremy said briefly.

Cressida put out a tentative hand. 'How do you do, Mrs. Bolton. I'm afraid—' She couldn't yet take in the overpowering figure before her, and her timid words were immediately interrupted.

'But it's unbelievable! It isn't true! She's—Jeremy, where did you find her?'

'At the bottom of your front steps, to be quite accurate. They are a deathtrap, as I've always said.'

'My husband liked them,' Arabia Bolton said. 'He said marble steps gave one a certain distinction. But this girl, Jeremy. She's exactly—tell me, child, what is your name?'

It was no use trying to take in the woman in front of her. Her vision was too uncertain. Surely this Mrs. Bolton, whoever she was, was not wearing a sparkling tiara at a slightly tipsy angle!

'Cressida Barclay,' she replied obediently.

'What else?' the imperious voice demanded.

'Cressida Lucy. The same as the advertisement.'

And then, most astonishing of all, she was wrapped in a suffocating embrace.

'My dear child! You're the answer to a prayer. If only you knew!'

The excited voice went on over her head. 'Do you know, Jeremy, I've had a dozen applicants, impostors all!'

'How do you know they were impostors?' Jeremy enquired mildly.

'Because they didn't look the part. Cressida

18

Lucy is young, fair, innocent. She's this girl. It's amazing. It's—oh, dear. I don't think I can stand it. Poor Lucy! Poor, poor Lucy!'

The surprising old woman was actually shedding tears. Her large, dark, beautiful eyes filled, and presently the drops spilled over and ran down her craggy cheeks. After a moment she wiped them impatiently away. She took out a handkerchief and blew her large prominent nose. Then she was smiling again, a most compelling warmth filling her face so that one no longer saw its age and bony ugliness.

'Away with the past!' she exclaimed dramatically. 'We're concerned with the present. It's so full of promise. Once I thought I could not live without camels and sand and heat and vultures, but there are other things, many other things. Come, my dear, and I'll show you the flat.'

Cressida made a final protest.

'But I can't stay here, really. I've no job, and I've spent my last penny.'

'Then my dear child, we must find you a job. What do you say, Jeremy?'

'First she needs food,' Jeremy said briefly.

'Ah, yes, of course. What are you giving her?'

'Bacon and eggs.'

'Very good. If you will invite me, I will share them with you. While you are busy I will look at this pretty child.'

Cressida's alarm, vague at first because of the lingering fumes of brandy, increased. When she had first come to look at this house two days ago, some instinct had made her leave without lifting the heavy dragon-shaped knocker on the front

19

door. She had been filled with some indefinable fear that later, as her straits grew more desperate, she had dismissed with determined scorn. Now she was sure that that fear had been justified. There was nothing at the moment that she wanted more than to be out of the house and in the streets, homeless perhaps and penniless, but free.

It was as if Jeremy Winter read her thoughts. From behind her his voice came reassuringly, as if everything, even the strange old woman fixing her large compelling eyes on her, were completely normal.

'Don't let Arabia upset you, Cressida. All you do is remind her of her daughter who died.'

CHAPTER THREE

It was astonishing how food brought the odd situation into an almost normal perspective. Cressida suddenly found herself thinking quite sanely. The circumstances were quite simple, and more pathetic than anything else. Arabia Bolton had had a beautiful daughter, Cressida Lucy, who had died at the pitiful age of only twenty-one. For years Arabia had cherished her grief, but now, in her old age, she had suddenly decided that life must be made to give back to her what it had taken away. In all her seventy-five years she had done a great many odd and fantastic things, and had a lot of desires granted her. But this, she said, with tears gleaming again in her great hooded eyes, was the most unexpectedly and perfectly fulfilled wish of them all.

For Cressida was astonishingly like her long-dead daughter. She was fair and young, she had that look of innocence and sweetness.

'My dear, you will stay, won't you? I'll find you a job, and I'll charge you just a little rent for the flat, so that you can keep your pride. For I know you have pride, just as my darling Lucy had. All I want is to see you now and then, to have youth in the house, to tell myself that Lucy didn't really die . . .'

'She must write to Tom,' came Jeremy Winter's voice from behind them.

Arabia's head shot up suspiciously.

'Tom?'

'He's my fiancé,' Cressida explained, with dignity.

'And do you intend to marry him?'

'Of course.'

A shadow passed across Arabia's face. Briefly her heavy eyelids drooped. Then she said firmly, 'But not for some time. You're much too young.'

'In June 1957,' Jeremy put in. 'Tom is a patient man.'

'He—he plans things,' Cressida said defensively.

Arabia's face suddenly sparkled with humour. It made Cressida think of sunlight on a wrinkled and sun-faded leaf. She had an unwilling feeling of magnetism. No one person, she thought, especially no one the age of this old woman, should have so many moods and so much colour and vitality. Cressida, who was kind-hearted and sensitive, would have found it difficult to disappoint any old person, but Arabia was not just

21

an ordinary old woman. She was long accustomed to getting her own way, and it was a foregone conclusion that Cressida would have been unable to disappoint her, even had she dreaded the thought of staying in Dragon House and playing the part of the dead-and-gone Lucy.

But now, with food comfortably inside her, she was no longer foolishly superstitious and afraid. After those two past dreadful days she had fallen on her feet. She had found a temporary haven, and, most important of all, she didn't need to go humbly back to Tom, confessing that he had been right and she wrong. He would have been so unbearably smug. Somehow, before she married him, she had to prove to him that she too had a mind and taste and discrimination. He had too long thought of her as an amenable child to be humoured and indulged, but not to be treated as a mental equal. This was her opportunity to prove him wrong, and in doing so to make their love much stronger and deeper.

She would do this, and at the same time make a lonely old woman happy. It seemed very simple and straightforward, and all at once she was very happy about it.

Arabia was leaning forward, her tiara threatening to fall over her eyes, her face alight with interest.

'Tell me about this Tom.'

'He's an accountant.'

Arabia nodded wisely. 'Ah, yes. Figures. Totting up columns. That explains the planning. A methodical mind. Will you be good at balancing your housekeeping money?'

'I shouldn't think so. I'm forgetful.'

22

'Tut, tut. That's one difficulty you will have to overcome. Marriage is a series of overcoming difficulties. Did you know that? My first husband used to expect me to jump fences every morning at the crack of dawn. I just couldn't stand it, especially liking camels so much better than horses. Now it never worried me to mount my camel and set off over the sand dunes in the fresh morning air—ah, how wonderful that was. But I don't suppose camels will come into your marriage, my dear.'

'Mrs. Bolton was married to an explorer,' came Jeremy's calm voice in the background.

'How interesting,' Cressida said, in some bewilderment.

'That was my third husband,' Arabia said. Her eyes began to brood. 'We went everywhere—Egypt, the Arabian desert, Tibet, Mongolia, the old silk route to China. Ah, life was rich. You must come upstairs and see my relics. But first let us dispose of this methodical Tom.'

Cressida, who had thought her sanity and clear-headedness had come back, was now floundering again. She had a bewildering feeling that Tom, sensible, matter-of-fact, level-headed Tom, was going to become one of this fantastic old woman's relics, which no doubt already included camels and dead husbands.

'She must write to him,' said Jeremy again. 'That is, of course, providing she has decided to stay.'

'But of course she is going to stay. We are going to find her a job. What can you do, my dear?'

'I write a little,' said Cressida. 'I'm good with

flowers. I can make my own clothes if I have to. I know quite a lot about antiques. I'm afraid this all sounds very ineffectual. Everyone I went to in London thought so. They expected me to be at least a debutante or to have a university degree.'

The old lady's hand, which was surprisingly strong and broad, and the thick square fingers of which were covered with rings, came down triumphantly on Cressida's knee.

'Mr. Mullins! The very man.'

'Is he?' said Jeremy doubtfully.

'But of course. I've been his best customer for years. When I'm not buying from him I'm selling to him, and of course he cheats me right and left, the old scoundrel. But I adore him. He's the very man.'

'What is he?' Cressida asked uncertainly.

'An antique dealer. He has the dustiest shop in London. I've been telling him for years that he must employ someone to brighten things up. Cressida is exactly the person he wants. And if she likes antiques, how she'll adore his collection. Now for the letter.'

'The letter?' Cressida's mind was struggling once more in the backwash of Arabia's volubility.

'To the methodical Tom. What shall she say, Jeremy? Shall she say she has another interest of the heart?'

Jeremy's eyebrow lifted into its crescent shape.

'That, I fear, is not strictly true. As yet.'

'No, but I think this Tom deserves a fright. He sounds too smug, like my first husband.'

Abruptly Cressida gave a smothered laugh. She found herself liking this strange and unpredictable old woman very much.

24

'Actually he is, a little. But I never tell him lies, Mrs. Bolton.'

'Call me Arabia, dear child. Lucy always did, although I was her mother. You're quite right, you shouldn't tell lies unless absolutely necessary, and then only white ones. Never mind, we shall think of something to say to Tom. Now I am going to take her from you, Jeremy. She is mine, not yours.'

Jeremy Winter gave the smile that turned his face into deep lines and shadows. His eyes gleamed brightly

'She is mine to draw. That's why I brought her in.'

Cressida had a flash of temper. 'Otherwise you would have left me lying in the street?'

'Perhaps I would have called a taxi.'

Arabia patted Cressida's arm.

'He thinks of nothing but his wicked pencil. If he annoys you or makes you fall in love with him I will give him notice.'

Cressida took a quick backward look at the dark, laughing face of Jeremy Winter.

'I am already in love,' she said with dignity.

'Ah, yes, my dear. To your balance sheet. Very wise, very safe. You hear that, Jeremy? You have her on paper only. And Tom has her in envelopes with postage stamps. At present she really belongs to me. And Lucy.'

★　　　★　　　★

It was much later that Cressida actually began the letter to Tom. She had meant to write him a polite but cool and reserved letter, because their

25

quarrel and Tom's obstinate smugness still rankled. But she was a natural writer, and it was not long before the reserve vanished, and her excited thoughts came pouring on to the paper.

'My dear Tom,

I promised to write when I was safely settled in London, and now I am able to do so. I have had the extraordinary last few hours. I had read an advertisement about a flat in a house belonging to an extraordinary old woman called Arabia Bolton. I will tell you presently how I got the flat, but first I must describe Arabia.

She is the most incredible, fascinating, bewildering, comic old woman. She lives on the top floor of this house, among an amazing conglomeration of things. One of her husbands (she had three) was an explorer, and they gathered every kind of bizarre thing on their travels, and now Arabia says she has brought all the world into a London room. She has two parrots, one live and one stuffed. There are Chinese ivories, enormous Indian brass trays, a pair of elephant's tusks over the door, drapings of Burmese silks on the couches, a Bedouin sheik's headdress hanging askew over an African death mask. I can't begin to tell you everything. And in the midst of all this Arabia sits like a queen, a slightly tipsy one because of her crooked tiara.

But I must come to the point of the story. Arabia had one child, a daughter, who was the darling of her heart but who, tragically, died when she was twenty-one, just before she was to be married. This is all about twenty years ago, and at first Arabia travelled furiously about the world to forget her grief. She lived in villages in the desert, and rode camels (she has a passion for them), and made friends with the Bedouins, and visited places like Baghdad and Istanbul. But now she is too old to do that any more, and she has had to stay at home and grow more and more dull and sad.

Then the other day she thought suddenly that there was no need to be lonely and unhappy. Life doesn't have to be dull. There are always ways to liven it up. The best way to do this is to try to get your heart's desire, even though it seems impossible. Lucy, her dead daughter, was Arabia's heart's desire, and I admit that to get her back was impossible.

But Arabia is the kind of woman who never admits that anything is unattainable. She had the brilliant idea of advertising her downstairs flat to let to a girl called Cressida Lucy—her daughter's names, and mine! Do you see the extraordinary coincidence? Because Arabia says that not only have I Lucy's size and colouring, but I am almost the age she was when she died.

This does not mean that Arabia is expecting me to stay with her forever. She just wants me to live in her house for a while, talk to her sometimes, and bring back an illusion of Lucy's youth and innocence.

So how could I refuse her? Apart from being terribly sorry for her she is an absolute poppet, and I adore her already. Also, I like being here, and I'm just so excited about going to work for Mr. Mullins, a friend of Arabia's, who has an antique shop. The whole thing sounds

27

extraordinarily like fate, don't you agree?

A word about the other people in the house. A funny little woman like an owl who thrust a note 'You're too late!' into my hand as I arrived, isn't something out of a melodrama. She has rooms upstairs, and she has some kind of throat trouble that means she can't speak above a whisper. She carries a pad and pencil with her all the time. When she wrote that message she thought the flat had been let, as someone had come earlier in the day. She lives with her son Dawson who is fifteen, is tall and thin and wears glasses, and isn't at all attractive. But I never did like precocious-looking children.

Miss Glory, a sea captain's daughter, lives in the ballroom and does the cleaning, and the other tenant on the ground floor is a violinist who plays in a night-club orchestra. His name is Vincent Moretti, and he has very light-coloured hair and eyebrows, so that he has almost a naked look. He flirts with Miss Glory, but I don't think he is really in love with her. She is flat and brown, like a piece of cardboard. But he makes jokes with her and she giggles. Obviously she adores him. His taste in music is rather macabre, but I expect he gets tired of playing dance music all night. So I will just have to endure elegies and laments during the day.

That is all, except Jeremy Winter who catches burglars in the basement. He is a commercial artist, and he is very self-assured and not at all my type.

Arabia has promised to tell me all of Lucy's

story, and this is going to give me the material for the long serious work that I have always wanted to do. It is so sweet and sad. There is this lovely young girl, full of gaiety and charm, going to balls, having lots of admirers, petted and pampered by her mother, wearing exquisite clothes, always laughing, and then suddenly falling sick and dying. Invitations to dances and parties were coming in after she was dead. They dressed her in her new ball gown and pinned on a corsage of flowers as if she were really going to a ball. Then Arabia kept her room exactly as it was when she died, with invitation cards and photographs on the dressing-table, her bed turned down, her night gown and slippers put out. Just as if she were going to be back from a party at any moment.

Arabia says I am to go in this room whenever I feel like it, and look at anything I want to. I am not being morbid. It is just that Lucy's life runs through this house like a remembered perfume, or a snatch of song.

My love and a thousand kisses.

Your Cressida.'

CHAPTER FOUR

In the middle of the night Cressida woke. Already she had slept only from exhaustion. Her excitement was stirring just beneath her consciousness, and the two hours' sleep that took away the acuteness of her tiredness brought intense awareness of her whereabouts back.

She lay for a little while listening to the quiet house. The music and the footsteps had ceased. First there had been Vincent Moretti's violin, as he had practised in his room at the back of the house before leaving for the night club from which he did not return until almost dawn. There had been some giggling in the passage as he stopped to chat to Miss Glory, and then, as if cheered by Mr. Moretti's passing remarks, a rollicking polka had come from the ballroom. That would be Miss Glory performing on the grand piano.

When the music had stopped there had been the sound of Mimosa's miaows as he prowled about the staircase. He was an uncommonly vociferous cat.

Later the front door had banged, and swift, firm footsteps had gone down the hall and towards the basement stairs. That was Jeremy coming in. Cressida had wondered idly if he had been taking a girl out, But if so he had left her very early. She was not interested in Jeremy Winter's night life, she told herself drowsily. She was only grateful to him for picking her up off the street and carrying her inside. Otherwise she would have run away from Dragon House and never have known about this pretty flat that Arabia was so delighted for her to have. It was unbelievable luck. It would be no hardship to spend most of her spare time with Arabia, who was so fascinating and interesting a person anyway, and to be rewarded with a delightful flat as well was too good to be true.

Arabia had said that after the last tenant had departed she had redone the rooms in preparation

30

for the arrival of a young girl. The paint was gay and fresh, the chintzes new, the carpets a warm, deep red. The bedroom had been done in yellow because that had been Lucy's favourite colour. But it had not been a deliberate copy of Lucy's room on the top floor of the house. Lucy was not to steal all the new Cressida Lucy's personality.

Had Cressida felt a faint shiver of apprehension at that remark of Arabia's? Of course she had not. She was herself, and not even required to play a part.

Nevertheless, as she lay in the dark, she kept thinking about that room at the top of the house, in its petrified state of awaiting the return of its owner from a ball.

She fell asleep thinking of it, and when she awoke it was still in her mind, compellingly. The turned-down bed, the little feathery slippers set demurely on the floor, the strewn and discarded jewellery on the dressing-table—nothing valuable: a young girl's seed pearls, a clip shaped like a bird, a comb studded with brilliants.

Arabia had taken her up there and had said she was to go up at any time she liked. No one else ever went there. Cressida could use Lucy's little walnut writing-table if she liked. Anything in that room was for her use.

There was nothing morbid about it, Arabia said. It was a sweet and happy room that made Lucy still alive. 'She's just terribly late coming home,' she said.

Arabia, standing there in her long formal dinner gown, the incongruous tiara perched rakishly on her white hair, was, indeed, a stranger figure than any charming little ghost coming home late from

31

a ball. Cressida had known then that she had to come to this room alone. Already Lucy's story was beginning to obsess her, and she knew that she had to write it. It might not have any great depth or drama, but it was so human, so charming, so pitiful. The young girl dancing her way unknowingly to death.

She wanted to sit in that room alone, to imagine herself into the dead Lucy, and then to write.

There had been a diary lying on the writing desk. As Cressida awoke in the middle of the night she was suddenly seeing that diary, tantalisingly unread. What was in it? No secrets, or it would not be there so innocently. But perhaps one would be able to read between the lines. Being Arabia's daughter, Lucy could not lack colour.

Cressida sat up in bed. The excitement, mounting tumultuously within her, would not let her sleep again. All at once she knew that she must go up to Lucy's room now, in the middle of the night, and learn her secrets.

As Tom constantly deplored, Cressida always acted on impulse. After all, it was impulse (and Tom's unendurable stubbornness) that had brought her to Dragon House and this rich untapped stream of material. She had the urge to explore that room upstairs at once, so she would do so.

Putting on her dressing-gown and slippers she set cautiously forth.

The marble steps that led to the front door of Dragon House continued in a broad imposing staircase to the first floor, where Arabia strewed her possessions in profusion through the large rooms overlooking the street, and the little dumb woman, Mrs. Stanhope, and her son Dawson, occupied the two smaller rooms at the back.

The top floor, which was semi-attic, had all been Lucy's. Two of the rooms were filled to overflowing with more of Arabia's vast and miscellaneous collection of furniture and outlandish trophies. The long low-ceilinged room at the back, with the balcony overlooking the narrow garden, was Lucy's bedroom.

The marble stairs stopped at the first floor. After that the steps were wooden, and covered with a thin dusty carpet. Cressida's footsteps sounded through the carpet, and the stairs were inclined to creak. She went very quietly because she didn't want to disturb anyone. She had to pass directly by Mrs. Stanhope's door, but she felt sure that, even disturbed, that timid little woman with the whispering voice wouldn't venture out. Neither would the gangling boy Dawson who had thrust out a bony hand to her when Arabia had introduced them, and afterwards had eyed her furtively, as if suspicious of her sudden arrival.

Cressida, who liked almost everybody, found it difficult to like Dawson because he seemed such a shy plain boy. But she was sorry for him, having to live this rather unnatural life with his voiceless little mother, and sorrier still for Mrs. Stanhope who seemed as nervous as a caught bird. She would be nice to those two, as well as to Arabia. After all, what would it cost her, she who suddenly had so much?

Life was so exciting. Cressida was reflecting on that as she groped her way up the last few steps, and went along the passage to Lucy's room. Then, as she softly opened the door and switched on the light, pity overcame her once more.

Why did Arabia torment herself with this room that looked so lived in? There were even fresh flowers on the dressing-table. Cressida stopped to look again at the photograph of Lucy taken at her coming of age. The young face had nothing of Arabia's hawk-like arrogance in it. It was soft and round, with its smiling mouth and halo of fine fair hair. The eyes were far-off, almost empty, as if dwelling on scenes far different from a photographer's studio. In the loosely clasped hands was a small bouquet of roses. Red roses had been Lucy's favourite flowers, Arabia had said.

It seemed to Cressida that their perfume was in the room, and all at once it made her think of death. She had to repress a shiver as she crossed to the writing-table and took up the diary which lay open at the last written page, as if waiting for the next entry. The writing was neat and feminine. The last words were, tragically, 'Dinner with Larry tonight and we talked about the wedding. Almost everything arranged now. Tomorrow must order the flowers...'

And that was all. The flowers had had to be ordered, indeed. But they had not been flowers for a wedding.

Cressida turned back the pages and read the light-hearted comments of a gay and popular girl. Dinners, dances, trips on the river, shopping, fittings for dresses, references to young men, Larry's name, of course, figuring predominantly. Only one entry had been scratched out. Cressida had to peer closely to decipher it. Was it 'Saw Monty tonight'? Who was Monty and why had his name been scratched out? The diary, which covered six months, bore no other reference to him. Was he too unimportant to be worthy of a permanent record, or had his behaviour been so unpleasant that Lucy had decided to forget it?

Apart from that one cryptic entry the diary told no secrets at all. Cressida put it down, resolving to ask Arabia tomorrow about the mysterious Monty.

Her curiosity took her to the wardrobe, and she began fingering the dresses hanging within. They were twenty years old, a pre-war style, but their prettiness and expensiveness were still apparent. She took out a ball dress in filmy green tulle, and was holding it against herself when she heard the faint sound at the door. Or had it been a sound?

As she listened there was nothing more. The pretty room, with its rose-shaded light, remained petrified, waiting for the return of its owner.

But suddenly Cressida had lost her taste for being there. All at once she felt morbid and lonely and sad. She had a sudden longing for Tom, and his solid, kindly face and reassuring smile. It was foolish of her to have come up here in the middle of the night. If she lingered, perhaps even her first unfounded fears about Dragon House would come back.

She would hurry back to bed, and the sanity that a sound sleep would bring.

She paused at the door to switch out the light, then turned the knob and found that the door was locked!

It couldn't be! After a moment, in which all her

35

apprehensive fear invaded her so that she was abruptly shivering, she switched on the light again and examined the door calmly. The lock must have caught. With a little manipulation it would open.

But it did not open. It really was locked. Cressida remembered now the faint sound she had heard. It must have been someone turning the key—someone who had crept silently up the stairs, knowing she was there.

This was absurd, of course. What possible satisfaction could anyone get from locking her in a dead girl's room? It must be a mistake.

But Cressida, remembering the furtive sound at the door knew soberly that it was not a mistake. Someone, either mischievously or maliciously, had decided to lock her into Lucy's room.

It was not a joke to be appreciated, and she did not intend to take it calmly. She began, without hesitation, to bang on the door and call out.

'Whoever is out there—come and open this door! I don't intend to stay here all night. Come along, please!'

Then she waited. There was no sound. It might have been that she was the only person in the whole house. Here she stood in this charming petrified room, the only thing alive...

Impatiently, and trying to control her panic, Cressida banged on the door again. Then she tried rapping with her heel on the floor, but the thick carpet muffled this sound. She went to the window and threw it open, and stepped on to the narrow balcony with its elaborate wrought-iron railing intertwined into the shape of vine leaves. It was a long way down to the narrow strip of garden. Leaning over, she could see that all the windows of the house were dark. No one on this side kept a solitary vigil, chuckling at the thought of the girl locked in the room upstairs. What lights would be showing on the other side? Arabia's? Miss Glory's, from her lonely splendour in the ballroom? Perhaps Jeremy Winter's, but they, deep in the basement, would not show.

The room directly under this was one of Arabia's. At this time Arabia would be in her bedroom, sleeping, no doubt, and probably deaf to any calls. Next to her rooms were those of Mrs. Stanhope and Dawson, but they too might possibly be out of earshot and sound asleep.

There was someone awake, of course. That was the person who had crept up the stairs and locked her in. It suddenly occurred to Cressida that what she was doing was probably exactly what that person had hoped for and, in a nasty sadistic way, was enjoying. Probably whoever it was liked to scare a girl and hoped she would presently have hysterics.

That, she could have told the practical joker, was one thing she never had, and even a night alone in this room would not give them to her. If it came to that, what was so impossible about spending a night here? The room was comfortable, even luxurious. By daylight she would have no difficulty in attracting anyone's attention. Miss Glory would be pottering in and out of the garden. Arabia or Mrs. Stanhope would hear her calling. It was only a matter of passing the hours until daylight, and those could best be passed in sleep.

Cressida hesitated only a moment before

stretching out on the turned-down bed. She did not get between the sheets. Something—was it the thought of sacrilege?—stopped her from doing that. She lay rather stiffly on the coverlet, and switched off the rosy bedside light.

But then the darkness leapt on her. The silence was so deep it was terrifying. No, it wasn't completely silence. There was a creaking sound. Or was there? Had she imagined it? Listen! Was that a faint padding? No—yes, what was that? A faint far-off crying sound. Oh, a cat miaowing. Mimosa, of course. Why was Mimosa prowling about the house? Wasn't he shut in with his master at night?

Or was it that his master, too, prowled ... *What was that?* It sounded like a voice hissing, 'Usurper!' And then a faint choking sound, as if someone were sobbing...

Cressida sat upright. She was aware of that delicate lingering scent of roses. She felt the silk of the carefully laid-out robe beneath her fingers. Suddenly she sprang off the bed, rigid with distaste.

How could she lie there on Lucy's bed, which awaited only Lucy who would never come again? Oh, it was not only sad and tragic, it was somehow unpleasant, as if her own warm blood were congealing, and she too was to be petrified into everlasting youth.

She couldn't stay in this room after all. It was too haunted. Somehow she had to get out, and not by way of the stairs where her tormentor was no doubt waiting to further enjoy her distress. Surely there must be a way over the balcony.

She was not without resourcefulness. She was

38

athletic enough even to shin down a drainpipe, if need be.

But that feat, to her great delight, Cressida found to be unnecessary. For leading down from the side of the balcony was a fire escape. Why hadn't she thought of looking for that before? This was as easy as could be. Even with her long dressing-gown she had no difficulty in descending the iron rungs to the terrace far below. She was even chuckling with amusement. Whoever had played that humourless joke on her had come off worst, after all.

Or had they? For, safely on the terrace, Cressida found that she could not get back into the house. All the doors were locked, and when she rather timidly tapped on Vincent Moretti's window, which was the only one to face the garden, there was no answer. Apparently he was not yet home.

But thank goodness there was a crack of light showing from the basement windows. Cressida shrugged resignedly. Once more she had to depend on Jeremy Winter for succour.

A steep flight of stairs led down to the back door. Cressida went down them quickly and banged briskly on the door.

Presently it opened and Jeremy stood there. He was fully dressed, but his black hair was rumpled as if he had been running his hand feverishly through it, and he looked sleepy. Mimosa was twisting voluptuously round his ankles.

Cressida said apologetically, 'Yours was the only light showing. That's why I knocked.'

'Did you, indeed?' Jeremy's dark eyes were losing their sleepy look. They swept over her appraisingly.

'It was the only way I could get in,' Cressida explained.

'And why not the way you got out?'

'That was down the fire escape.' Abruptly Cressida, who was beginning to shiver, lost her politeness and said sharply, 'Aren't you going to let me in? I've had enough practical jokes for one night. I suppose it was you who locked me in Lucy's room, too.'

Suddenly she was remembering Mimosa's calling on the stairs, and her gaze took in Jeremy's fully dressed appearance. Why was he still up? It was after two o'clock.

But now she had his interested attention.

'You don't mean you've been locked in that room?'

'And what do you think I would be doing here dressed like this if I hadn't?'

He gave her tart question serious consideration.

'Actually I don't know you very well.'

'Oh, don't be idiotic. You know me well enough to know I wouldn't be climbing down fire escapes in my dressing-gown from preference.'

'But why should anyone lock you in? The door must have jammed. Look here, I'll just sprint upstairs and see. Come and sit by my fire. You're cold.'

Cressida wrapped her arms round herself. 'I'm not cold. It's just that room at night. I shouldn't have gone up alone. I felt as if someone were walking over my grave.'

But she was talking to herself, for Jeremy had already gone. As she walked into his living-room, brightly lighted, and with his drawing-board

40

prominently placed, she could hear his quick footsteps, growing more muffled as he reached the top of the house. In a very short time he was down again.

He looked at Cressida a moment, the expressive eyebrow almost in his hair. Then he said, quite calmly,

'The door wasn't locked. There isn't even a key.'

'Oh, but it was! I swear—' She was aware of his completely sceptical gaze. Her quick temper sprang out. 'Jeremy Winter, do you stand there thinking I made that excuse to come down the fire escape in my dressing-gown just to see you? Oh no, surely you couldn't flatter yourself that much.'

'Too bad,' Jeremy murmured.

'I won't stand it!' Cressida cried. 'I expect the truth is that you went up just now and unlocked the door. After all, I did hear Mimosa on the stairs when I was in Lucy's room.'

'Mimosa!' Jeremy said accusingly. 'Did you lock the lady in? Naughty creature!'

'Don't be idiotic!' Cressida was nearly beside herself with anger, and that humiliating lingering fear. 'I was locked in that room tonight, and if I hadn't come down the fire escape I would have had to spent the night there. Somebody pretended not to hear me calling, and then, I suppose, seeing or hearing me go down the fire escape, rushed upstairs to unlock the door and pretend nothing had happened.'

'Sit down,' said Jeremy. 'You're still shivering.'

'No, I won't sit down. This isn't a social call. Thank you for letting me in, and now I'll go.'

Jeremy made no move to go and open the door.

41

'You're very attractive when you're angry. Does Tom think so?'

'Please leave Tom's name out of this.'

'I can't very well, because at this moment I'm wondering if you wouldn't be wise to go home to him after all, pride or no pride.'

Mimosa suddenly rubbed insinuatingly round Cressida's ankles. Cressida looked down at his broad golden back, and then up at the tall young man in front of her. He was not laughing now. He was looking at her quizzically, even with something like seriousness. She found her anger leaving her.

'Why do you say that?'

'Because here, whatever else you may be, I'm afraid you're going to be someone come back from the grave. And already, you see, it isn't particularly healthy.'

'You don't mean—Arabia?' Cressida was almost whispering. She had a sudden vision of being a prisoner forever in that charming lifeless room, her only visitor the old woman in her outlandish clothes.

Jeremy looked genuinely puzzled. 'Actually I can't believe she would do a crazy thing like that. I know she thoroughly enjoys romancing, and being amusing, and shocking, if possible, but I always thought she was quite sane. Look here, you'd better go to bed and convince yourself you dreamed the thing. I'll take you upstairs.'

'I didn't dream it,' Cressida said soberly. 'And I don't intend to go home to Tom either. At least, not yet. Getting locked in either accidentally or on purpose doesn't frighten me. Lucy's story is just the kind of thing I have been looking for, and I

42

intend to find out more of it. I'm sure there's more to find out. Who was Monty in her diary, for instance?'

'Just debutante stuff,' Jeremy said.

'Perhaps. But Arabia gets a look in her eye. I don't think she's telling me everything. And as for you'—she turned on him suddenly—'what are you doing up at this hour of night?'

'Working,' said Jeremy mildly. 'I do a strip cartoon featuring Mimosa. Like to see it?'

He indicated his drawing-board, and Cressida looked with amusement at the rows of plump cats, walking stiffly on their hind legs, holding animated conversations.

'Mimosa is a bit slow in providing me with a plot sometimes,' Jeremy complained. 'He's a lazy brute.'

Cressida laughed involuntarily. Then suddenly she was remembering again Mimosa's miaow on the stairs and the furtive sound at the door. Had this all been an elaborate scheme to stimulate a jaded imagination? No, that was foolish ... Unless Jeremy had thought it would be amusing to have her come to his door so late at night, knowing she would inevitably come down the fire escape.

'They're supposed to be funny,' Jeremy observed.

'Oh, they are, too. I like them.'

'Well, don't scowl like that. Come and I'll take you to your room. There's Mimosa gone ahead. He's skittish enough at two o'clock in the morning.'

Indeed, Mimosa had darted ahead, surprisingly fleet and silent for so large a cat. When they reached Cressida's door he was there first, and as

43

Jeremy leaned forward to open it, whispering, 'Not a sound or your reputation has gone, the house is full of old women,' Mimosa darted into the room.

'Blast that animal!' Jeremy exclaimed.

'Oh, come in and catch him,' Cressida laughed. She switched on the light, and had a sensation of renewed pleasure at the sight of the bright, attractively furnished room. 'There he is under the couch. If I go on this side—what are you looking at?'

Jeremy was looking at the table. He was looking at a key—large, old-fashioned and a little rusted. Under it was a sheet of paper and on the paper was printed cryptically: *But the grave has no need of a key.*

CHAPTER FIVE

'You put it there!' Cressida burst out.

Jeremy lifted his brows. 'You think so?' he said. That was all.

Why had he this way, with his quiet amusement, of making her feel young and foolish, particularly foolish? He annoyed her extremely, and it was unfortunate indeed that she had been so dependent on him.

'Who else could it be? Everyone else is in bed asleep.'

'How do you know? Have you looked?'

'Don't be absurd! One can't go unceremoniously into other people's rooms.'

'Someone has had no qualms about coming

44

unceremoniously into yours.'

Then Jeremy patted her shoulder in a paternal way, and said,

'Don't worry any more about it tonight. It's an unpleasant joke, but harmless. Go to bed and get some sleep. All right?'

Cressida nodded reluctantly. She should have been glad to see him go, but that lurking intuitive fear had come back, and suddenly she dreaded being alone.

'At least you know now that I didn't imagine the door was locked.'

'Your reputation is unblemished, my dear. I'll do some snooping tomorrow. Now get some sleep or you'll be useless to me as a model. I'm not accustomed to drawing circles under beautiful eyes.'

She suspected then that he was not so much being impertinent as joking to cheer her up. But when he had gone all her apprehension returned. Someone didn't like her being in this house. And it was someone who was jealous of Lucy's memory. Who could it be, after all, but Arabia?

Surprisingly enough Cressida did sleep soundly for the remainder of the night, and awoke only to the peremptory tap of Miss Glory on her door.

'You still asleep?' she said in her abrupt way. 'I thought you might like a cup of tea, as I don't expect you've had time to get in any provisions yet.'

Cressida sat up, welcoming the tall angular woman with the sallow face, dragged-back hair and slightly forbidding manner. She was being very kind, and the abruptness of her voice probably hid shyness.

45

'Thank you very much,' she was beginning, when a voice down the hall called,

'Where are you, rosebud, my own?'

Miss Glory giggled suddenly and surprisingly. Her brown eyes had grown soft.

'That's Mr. Moretti. Isn't he absurd. Rosebud, indeed! He does it because he knows it makes me angry.'

But Miss Glory wasn't angry. She was faintly blushing.

'Will you be going out this morning, Miss Barclay?'

'Yes, I have to see about a job.'

'Then I'll do you while you're out.'

'But I don't think I can afford to pay—'

Miss Glory jerked her head towards the ceiling. 'Say no more. Orders from above. You're the pet.'

'Oh, but—'

'I shouldn't worry. Take all you can. You'll pay in another way, just as I do.' Miss Glory's voice was cryptic. 'Did you sleep well?'

Cressida hesitated. She looked at the sallow, angular face, and instantly dismissed the thought that Miss Glory could have had any interest in prowling about the house at night.

'Yes, thank you,' she said politely. 'And thank you very much for the tea.'

'You're welcome.' The softness momentarily came back into the brown eyes. 'It's nice to see a young face about.'

As the result of Miss Glory's thoughtful visit, Cressida's mercurial spirits soared again. *But the grave has no need of a key* ... Those words did not belong to this fine morning. They were part of last night's nightmare, and to be forgotten as a nightmare was on waking. She drank her tea, then sang as she bathed and dressed. The clatter of bottles announced the arrival of the milkman, and she went out to get her milk just as Mrs. Stanhope was saying goodbye to Dawson at the front door. Dawson, the tall gangling boy, stooped to kiss his mother, then saw Cressida and gave her a shy nod, not looking at her.

He was at the awkward stage, Cressida thought, and couldn't be criticised for his somewhat offhand manners, but she still could find nothing particular to like about him. He had a long, narrow head covered with spiky hair, his skin was pale, and his eyes behind thick glasses were myopic. Poor boy, he hadn't been endowed with much physical beauty, but obviously his mother doted on him, and obviously also he was a devoted son.

As Dawson went down the steps Mrs. Stanhope turned to come back indoors, and saw Cressida. She smiled with all the friendliness that her son had lacked. Her hand, with its instinctive movement, went to her throat. She whispered something inaudible.

She was very thin and small, and looked underfed. Dawson's skin was pale but it did not have the unhealthy pallor of his mother's. Mrs. Stanhope could not have been more than perhaps forty, but her fine straight hair was faded to an indeterminate colour, and her narrow pointed face set in deep lines. The large glasses, out of proportion to the size of her face, took away whatever personality she might have had.

Cressida's ready sympathy was becoming

47

involved once more. She wanted to know all about Mrs. Stanhope, and why she seemed so poor and ill. Doubtless she had a history of bad luck. Probably her husband had died young and she had been left with a son to feed and educate. As she was definitely the helpless type this would have been a severe struggle.

'Good morning, Mrs. Stanhope. Will you come in and see my flat?' Cressida asked.

Mrs. Stanhope nodded eagerly. 'That's very kind of you,' she whispered. 'I'm so glad Mrs. Bolton didn't let it to that other woman yesterday, as I thought she had. You're so young and pretty. It's nice for all of us.'

Inside the flat she nodded and smiled as Cressida showed off her things. Then, clutching her throat in her automatic gesture, she whispered, 'I'm not supposed to talk much,' and bringing out her pad and pencil she wrote, 'I hope you will let Dawson and me be your friends.'

Cressida was moved by her kindness. Why had she ever thought Dragon House was a sinister and unfriendly place? Everyone was making particular efforts to be kind. Except the person who had played that morbid joke on her last night...

'Mrs. Stanhope,' she said impulsively, 'did you hear anything last night some time after midnight? Like someone prowling on the stairs?'

The little woman looked alarmed, her eyes huge behind the heavy glasses.

'Burglars?' she whispered.

'No, not burglars. Someone snooping.' Suddenly she decided to tell the whole story. 'I went up to Lucy's room and while I was there someone locked me in.'

48

Mrs. Stanhope gasped, her hand at her throat. Then she took her pencil and pad and wrote very decisively, 'It would be Arabia.'

'Arabia?' Cressida said unbelievingly.

Mrs. Stanhope wrote furiously, 'Arabia is kind and charming, but she is unbalanced where Lucy is concerned. I think you should be careful.'

'Careful of what?' Cressida exclaimed.

'Her eccentric ways,' Mrs. Stanhope wrote. 'She may begin to hate you because you are alive and Lucy is dead.'

Then she smiled apologetically, and whispered, 'Perhaps I imagine this. But I'm in the house all day and I notice things.'

'I don't believe Arabia would hurt a fly,' Cressida said warmly.

Mrs. Stanhope gave her her myopic stare. Then she shrugged her thin shoulders and wrote, 'Who else would do a thing like that?' After a pause she continued, 'If I were you I wouldn't dabble too much in Lucy's story.'

There was a great deal of sense in what Mrs. Stanhope suggested, and she had been living here long enough to be aware of Arabia's ways. Cressida didn't know why she found the thought of Arabia's being the practical joker so hurtful and distasteful. She had liked the old lady so much the previous evening. She had been captivated by her warmth and colour and vitality.

Would a silly joke like that spoil her liking? Cressida was afraid it would, but she was wrong, for the instant Arabia appeared at her door half an hour later she was swept into the spell of that unique personality.

Ahmed, the grey and rose-coloured parrot, was

perched on her shoulder. Arabia wore, not the dramatic black velvet of the previous evening but a very old and worn tweed suit and a battered felt hat perched rakishly on her very erect head. She looked like an eccentric duchess setting out for some village gathering, except that Ahmed did not fit into any conventional picture.

'Good morning, my love,' she said to Cressida in her rich warm voice. 'Did you sleep well in your new surroundings?'

'Yes, I—'

'Excellent, excellent. So did I. That is one blessing that is left to me. The ability to sleep soundly. I fear I won't even wake on the Day of Judgment. My dear, you look so fresh and pretty. But then at your age one does. Even after dancing all night Lucy could look like a freshly opened buttercup in the morning. Now we're on our way to Mr. Mullins. Are you ready?'

Had Arabia crept about the house in the night, locking doors furtively, and chuckling and sobbing? Or had she truly slept soundly, as she said? There was no guile in those handsome, heavy-lidded eyes. Cressida was sure that she was speaking what she believed to be the truth. It could be, however, that she had lapses of memory, or even that she sleepwalked. If the joke had been played unconsciously, it was not so unpleasant.

Cressida decided abruptly to put it out of her mind, and to plunge whole-heartedly into this exciting new day.

Arabia suggested walking, as Mr. Mullins's shop was not more than two blocks away in Gloucester Road. She bundled Ahmed unceremoniously off her shoulder and told him to go home, which he proceeded to do by hopping from stair to stair in a clumsy sideways manner, all the time grumbling raucously.

'He always asks to be taken out,' Arabia said. 'Some day I shall have to humour him. Isn't he beautiful—those pearl-grey feathers, like early dawn over the desert. I adore parrots, don't you? So much more attractive than vultures, and there have been plenty of *those* in my life.' She gave Cressida her dazzling smile, that gave that strange illusion of youth and beauty to the craggy old face, and tucked her arm in Cressida's. 'Now, my dear, as we go along you must tell me your life story. Where are your parents, where do you live, how did you come to meet this balance-sheet Tom?'

Cressida obediently related briefly that she lived in a Cotswold town, that she had known Tom since she was a child (he had been almost grown-up while she was still a little girl, and that perhaps explained his habit of domination over her), that her parents were both dead, her father just recently, after which she had stayed on in the family home, letting half of it to the resident schoolmistress. She had thought that after her father's death Tom would want to marry her at once, but he had cautiously kept to the original plan of buying and furnishing their home first.

'And letting you grow older and more responsible,' Arabia commented shrewdly. 'This Tom is taking no risks, I can see. Go on.'

To earn money, of which there was very little, Cressida worked on a small local newspaper, reporting weddings and social gatherings, which she found intensely boring, and which gave her no outlet at all for her creative talent. As well, she arranged flowers for parties, and did a little buying and selling of antiques, attending such auction sales as there were in neighbouring houses. That was all. She was always poor. She didn't know where money went. It slipped away, just as her life had been slipping away in that quiet town, with only Tom to give it his masterful direction.

'I was really suffering from frustration when we quarrelled,' she confessed.

'And my dear, do I wonder at it! Why, that was the life for an octogenarian. You must discover the world. It's so full of things. And money is the least, really. I am so glad you know that already. Ah, we'll have fun together. I shall start going to theatres again. And museums. And we might take a boat on the river, or go to Battersea fun-fair. Life! That's what we shall have.'

'Arabia,' said Cressida, 'who was Monty?'

She felt the old lady stiffen. Or had she just been bracing herself against a sudden sharp breeze—for her voice, when she replied, was as bland as ever.

'Monty? Never heard of him!'

'He was in Lucy's diary. The entry had been crossed out, but I could just read the name.'

'Then your eyes must be better than mine. I have never seen or heard of the name before. Lucy knew a lot of boys, of course. She was a very popular girl. If you look right through the diary you will find other names besides Larry's.

'Then if there were others, how are you so certain there was no Monty?'

52

'Because that's a most unlikely name for one of Lucy's friends to have had,' Arabia snapped. 'It might have been the name of one of her friends' dogs. That's what it sounds like.'

'Yes, of course,' Cressida agreed politely, knowing now that there had been a Monty, and that he had been someone whom Arabia had not liked. Perhaps he had been Lucy's one slip from perfection. At least that made her more human. Cressida's conviction that there was a story behind Lucy grew. The next time she went up to that empty bedroom she would take the precaution of removing the key from the door. In no other way would the practical joker intimidate her.

'And here we are,' Arabia said briskly, 'at Mr. Mullins's. Now come in and look your most charming. Albert is a cheat and a rascal, but I adore him.'

Mr. Mullins did not look either a cheat or a rascal. He was small and round, and he had a face like a Dresden cupid. He greeted Arabia with affection, wanting to hold her heavily ringed hand softly in his, but she impatiently snatched it away and plunged it into the large handbag she was carrying.

'Albert, I have brought you the Marie Antoinette clock, and a new assistant.'

Mr. Mullins's pink face dimpled with pleasure. His hands went out reverently for the crumpled brown parcel that Arabia produced.

'My dear lady! At last!'

'Don't be so avaricious,' Arabia said sharply. 'Take a look at your new assistant. Her name is Cressida Barclay, and she is living with me, and

53

she knows all there is to know, probably a great deal more than you do, about antiques.' Mr. Mullins put the small elaborate clock down and held out his plump hand to Cressida.

'How do you do, Miss Barclay. But how pretty she is Arabia.'

'Of course she's pretty. She'll look more attractive in your shop than all this junk you've got here.'

'Mr. Mullins may not need an assistant,' Cressida ventured.

'Of course he needs an assistant. I've been telling him so for years. Someone to dust, someone to mind the shop while he goes to lunch. He starves himself to death. Now, it's no use to deny that, Albert. I know it. Cheese sandwiches, indeed!'

Mr. Mullins nodded meekly.

'That is true. I do eat a great many sandwiches. And the dust certainly is a problem. To be quite truthful, Miss Barclay, I would have had an assistant long ago if I could have found the right person. Since Arabia assures me that you are—'

'There's no question about it, Albert.' Arabia's deep, compelling voice swept all doubt aside. 'Now give me your miserly pittance for the clock and I'll leave you to instruct Cressida in her duties.'

The two moved into the corner of the shop where the cash desk was, and after some wrangling, during which Arabia's voice saying, 'What a wretched old cheat you are!' emerged clearly, Arabia left, and Cressida was left in the dark shop with its fascinating dusty conglomeration of objects, and the cherubic Mr.

Mullins.

He was still reverently handling the little French clock.

'I've wanted this for years,' he said. 'Arabia would never sell. She's a most unpredictable person. On never gives up hope, because one day, just like this, she will change her mind.'

'Now you have the clock and me too,' Cressida said.

'To be quite honest, Miss Barclay, the bribe was unnecessary. I do need an assistant, and in fact I had been going to put a card in the window today. Here it is, written out. So one would almost call it fate.'

Or coincidence, thought Cressida. Were there being too many coincidences in her life at present for comfort?

'I think you will be very suitable, especially if you know even a little about antiques.'

'I do,' Cressida assured him.

'Then what could be better? Supposing you take a duster, and as you work you will get to know my stock. At first, please refer all customers to me, except for small articles that are plainly marked with the price.' He paused to give his dimpling smile. 'I think we should get along very well, Miss Barclay.'

So here was one more person who was being kind to her. All at once Cressida had an uncomfortable intuition to distrust her good fortune. It could not, surely, continue like this.

'Thank you, Mr. Mullins. I'll do my best.'

'I didn't ask your age, Miss Barclay, or where you come from.'

'I'm twenty-two and I come from the

Cotswolds.'

'And how long have you known Mrs. Bolton?'

'Only since yesterday. She has rather adopted me, I'm afraid. After all, how could one be unsympathetic—'

She stopped as she was aware of Mr. Mullins's sober and intense gaze.

'You are referring to the daughter, of course.'

'Yes, Lucy.'

'She's been dead a long time now.'

'But Arabia dotes on her.'

'It doesn't pay to dote too much on people.' Mr. Mullins closed his little mouth firmly and looked wise. Cressida suddenly wanted to smile at his earnestness.

'If I were you, Miss Barclay, I wouldn't let Arabia dote too much on you.'

'But why should she? I'm a complete stranger.'

'You remind her of Lucy. Didn't she tell you so?'

'Yes, she did.'

'She's a strange and impulsive woman. Oh, I'm not saying a word against her. She's one of my oldest and dearest friends. But she takes things hard.'

'Are you warning me about something, Mr. Mullins?'

'Only that over-possessiveness can be an uncomfortable thing.'

'Did you know Lucy?' Cressida asked eagerly.

Did his eyes flicker a moment? She couldn't be sure, for his countenance remained bland and cherubic.

'No, I'm sorry to say I didn't. That was before my friendship with Arabia began. Now, perhaps,

Miss Barclay, you could start in this corner. With the grandfather clock, eh? He has chimed sixty thousand days in and out, and he still isn't tired. That inlaid table is Chinese, and be very careful of the blue vase. It's of the Han Dynasty. But all my things are treasures. I hate to sell them, you know.'

Indeed, it seemed that selling his stock was of secondary importance to Mr. Mullins. For Cressida found that the dusting was going to be a herculean task. Behind the larger pieces of furniture were stacked innumerable smaller pieces, and behind them again pieces of pottery and brass, glass chandeliers, Victorian china and dim old pictures in heavy frames. Cressida emerged from her investigation to ask for a smock, and then, wrapped in an old blue cotton garment that belonged to the charwoman, she plunged enthusiastically into her work. She began to make discoveries—a Rockingham tea-set pushed into a cupboard, a pair of Staffordshire china cats that were ridiculously like Mimosa in their smug erectness, and then the exquisite Dresden mirror. With this she was enchanted, and she took it into the light at the doorway to clean and polish it thoroughly. The rosy cupids tossed garlands of flowers from their dimpled hands and these wove into lovers' knots at the base. Engrossed in her work, Cressida did not hear footsteps, and the voice above her startled her.

'Is that for sale?'

She looked up sharply and saw Jeremy Winter's dark, amused face.

'This mirror?'

'No, the face in it.'

57

Cressida looked down and saw her own face, her hair tousled, a smear of dust on her nose, her cheeks as rosy as the cupids'.

'Don't be absurd,' she retorted.

'It's the most charming upside-down face, I'm in love with it.'

'The mirror is very beautiful,' Cressida said, holding it up.

'Ah, but now it's empty. Who wants an empty mirror? Tell me, did Tom ever see you upside down in a mirror with dust on your nose? If he did he would never have let you go.'

'You can't come here wasting my time,' Cressida said impatiently.

Jeremy leaned lightly against the door.

'I'm expecting you this evening for a sitting. You will come, won't you?'

'Certainly not,' Cressida said, polishing vigorously.

'What, after my saving your life twice yesterday?'

'Oh, please go away!' Cressida begged. 'I work here, and Mr. Mullins—'

'Mr. Mullins is a friend of mine.' Jeremy waved casually to Mr. Mullins, who appeared from the back of the shop, grinned, and disappeared again tactfully. Cressida was furious with his tact. Did he think she wanted to be alone with Jeremy?

'He lends me things to sketch,' Jeremy explained. 'I did those T'ang lions last week. They made a wonderful background for my subject.'

'So you think he'll lend you me, also,' Cressida said scathingly. 'And what article am I supposed to be advertising?'

'Nothing,' said Jeremy simply. 'I just want to draw you for pleasure. I knew that the moment I saw you yesterday.' Then, as if ashamed of his lapse into seriousness, he added flippantly, 'I won't tell Tom.'

Cressida gave an exclamation of impatience. Jeremy touched her arm.

'Did anyone confess this morning about the fun they had playing tricks on you last night?'

'No, I'm afraid not. Mrs. Stanhope said—but I can't believe it.

'Believe what?'

'That Arabia does—curious things!'

'Then it must have been a poltergeist,' Jeremy said lightly. 'At Lucy's instigation.'

'Don't be idiotic!' Cressida was surprised at her breathlessness.

'If Lucy is around,' Jeremy said seriously, 'it might not be wise to use that pretty room of hers too much. She might get jealous. She might get jealous of Arabia's affection for you, too.'

'Jeremy, that's absurd! She's dead, dead.'

'Yes, indeed. So Arabia says. Are you going to sit for me tonight? For love?'

He grinned, lifting his mobile eyebrow into his hair, and then was gone, his footsteps down the street very quick and light. Cressida stood in forgetfulness of her surroundings, lost in the disturbing implication of his words. Did he really think that Lucy might not be dead? But why then the empty room, Arabia's twenty-year-long grief, the morbidly preserved fragments of Lucy's young life? Oh, no, that was a fantastic thing to suggest. It was a trick to get her down to his room, to persuade her to sit for him. He was a smooth and

59

clever schemer, he and that yellow cat of his...

'He is a handsome young man, isn't he?' came Mr. Mullins's soft approving voice.

Cressida spun round angrily.

'I don't think he is in the least. And I'll tell him not to come here wasting my time again.'

'Ah, but I don't mind a little wasted time. I'm not a slave-driver.' Mr. Mullins nodded his head gently. Why, he was nothing but a romantic and womanish matchmaker! The old fool!

'I happen to have a fiancé,' Cressida said stiffly. 'I shall be going home to be married after I have had some experience in London.'

'Experience is an enlightening thing,' Mr. Mullins observed. 'Ah, that mirror is exquisite. Shall we put it in the window? And the little French clock beside it. Do you know, this little clock was reputed to have been made especially for Marie Antoinette. It is a great treasure. Arabia valued it very much.'

'Mr. Mullins, you know Arabia.' The mysterious apprehension, like cool water, was flowing over her again. 'Should I not stay there, after all? Should I go home to Tom?'

Mr. Mullins took her hand in his own, which were soft, like pale-pink velvet.

'Don't hurry away, my dear. Just keep—shall I say emotions—in control? Be kind but firm. Arabia has suffered a lot. If she thinks she can get back what she lost, and if you think you can give it to her, then what are we alarmed about? And anyway, it is perfectly safe. You have that nice young man to look after you.'

60

CHAPTER SIX

When Cressida arrived home that evening the house was full of the strangest undercurrents of noise. Vincent Moretti was playing his violin in a slow dirge-like way. His door must have been open, for the muted wailing sounded quite clearly through the house. It had upset Mimosa, for he was stalking down the hall giving, at intervals, his raucous miaow, and somewhere overhead Miss Glory had an electric cleaner going. Added to this, Arabia had suddenly chosen to sing in a deep-carrying contralto something about flying on the wings of her desire.

Cressida unwrapped the fish she had brought home for her supper and heated a pan in which to cook it. She found herself unable to concentrate on what she was doing. The long exciting day had tired her. She wanted to write all about it to Tom, but at the same time the urge in her was to sit down and make notes about Lucy's story. There was the charming young girl who had died almost on the eve of her marriage, leaving the unfinished diary, the unanswered invitations, the room awaiting her return—as if she were not so much dead as absent for a while, a kind of invisible sleeping beauty. There was the mystery of the crossed-out line about someone called Monty, and the much more immediate mystery of who had played pranks with the key of the door.

'Dear Tom (Cressida wrote),
By this time you will have received my letter,

and I do hope that you are not still angry with me. I must stay here at present, because I am growing more and more absorbed in Lucy's story. I know that she died tragically young, but there is no suspicion that—'

'She was murdered!' came a sharp shrill voice.

Cressida leapt up. She had left her door ajar, and the voice came from the hall. Swiftly she was there, to see only Dawson Stanhope poring over an evening newspaper, making his slow progress to the stairs, while his mother impatiently signalled to him to hurry.

'In her dancing shoes,' Dawson continued in his morbidly excited voice. 'Red ones.'

'Lucy!' Cressida gasped.

Mrs. Stanhope's hand flew to her throat in its familiar nervous gesture. Then she clutched the banisters and seemed to sway.

Cressida ran up the stairs.

'Are you all right, Mrs. Stanhope?'

'Yes,' came the faint whisper. Then the little woman turned on Dawson, who stood grinning slightly in an ashamed way. 'You're a bad boy! You know how nervous I am. You shouldn't gloat over those things.'

'You mean it isn't Lucy you're talking about,' Cressida said.

Dawson gave a high-pitched giggle.

'It's this blonde in the paper. She was found on an empty bomb site strangled. She was wearing red shoes and an evening dress.'

Mrs. Stanhope had got out her pad and was writing feverishly. She handed the slip of paper to Cressida. 'Dawson has a legal mind,' it stated proudly.

Cressida tried to conceal her distaste for the overgrown boy with his unattractive features. She didn't like the way his eyes gleamed behind the thick glasses. His mother was a harmless and timid little owl, but he was of a more unpleasant species, and going through adolescence in a particularly unlikeable way. However, perhaps one should make allowances since he apparently hadn't a father, and his mother looked quite unable to cope with adolescent problems.

Mrs. Stanhope was continuing to scribble on her pad.

'He works for a chemist. If you require anything he will get it for you.'

Cressida nodded feebly, seeing in her mind's eye a row of bottles, all labelled 'Poison'. She could well imagine Dawson's pale face bending eagerly over some brew of his own concoction.

'He experiments sometimes,' Mrs. Stanhope wrote proudly.

'Not dangerously, I hope,' Cressida said.

Dawson gave his smug grin.

'Once I blew up Ma's kitchen and only singed my eyebrows. That was all, wasn't it, Ma?'

Mrs. Stanhope nodded with her blind, maternal pride.

'I'll do other shopping for you, if you like,' Dawson volunteered offhandedly. 'I do some for Mrs. Bolton when I do ours, and I could just as easily do yours, too.'

'He gets the groceries and vegetables,' Mrs. Stanhope wrote on her pad.

'Why, that's very kind of you,' Cressida said reluctantly.

'Just give me a list in the mornings,' said Dawson. 'I say, Ma, this girl lived in West Cromwell Road. That's not far from here. Why I might have passed the murderer in the street today.'

Mrs. Stanhope whispered, 'Please, Dawson!' She looked in distress at Cressida, then she wrote, 'It is dangerous for young girls alone in London.'

Cressida laughed gaily. 'Don't worry about me, Mrs. Stanhope. I'm very well able to look after myself.'

'But not after your fish!' came Jeremy's voice from the bottom of the stairs. 'Your kitchen's on fire.'

Cressida gasped, and flew down the stairs. 'Oh, dear, I forgot it!'

'So I gather. The smoke was coming down to me. I thought I had better investigate.'

Cressida, not stopping to speak to him, fled into her kitchen to see the blackened and pungent frying-pan rescued from the gas flame.

'What a lousy cook you are,' Jeremy's voice came from behind her.

Cressida's nerves, taut already from too much excitement, and from her vaguely disturbing encounter with the Stanhopes, snapped, 'Oh, will you stop interfering with my business! What does it matter to you what sort of cook I am?'

'It doesn't matter to me in the least. But I have a rather strong conviction that it does to Tom. He would like lightly grilled sole with a delectable sauce, no?'

It was so true a picture of Tom, who ardently liked good food well cooked, that Cressida's flash of temper increased.

'It's absolutely none of your business what Tom likes.'

'Even Mimosa,' Jeremy reflected, 'would turn up his nose at that fish. What else have you to eat?'

'Are you my guardian, or something?'

'I don't like my models to look half-starved, that's all.'

'In future,' Cressida snapped, 'my door will be kept shut.'

He was instantly serious and distant.

'I do apologise for bursting in like this, and spoiling your nice little outbreak of fire.'

Reluctantly Cressida had to smile.

'Oh, I'm sorry. I'm in a bit of a state. I thought this would be such a peaceful house, and it isn't at all. It's restless, and so uneasy, as if—'

'Yes?'

'Almost as if Lucy's ghost—' Cressida stopped, ashamed of her imagination. 'That murder in the paper tonight had absolutely no connection with anything here, and yet immediately I thought of Lucy. Why?'

'You are getting what is known as a writer's obsession.'

'It's as if every thought that is made in this house is about Lucy. A girl dead twenty years. It's fantastic.

'I frequently think of girls with other names,' Jeremy observed. He was wearing corduroy slacks and a green open-necked shirt. His hair was untidy, as usual, his eyes glinting with their familiar amusement. 'Now, look, if you haven't anything else to eat—'

If he had been going to offer Cressida another

meal of eggs and bacon he was too late, for at that moment Arabia grew vociferously nearer. '*I'll sing thee songs of Araby...*'

The song stopped at Cressida's door. There was a playful tap, and then Arabia's tiara-ed head was stuck coquettishly into the room.

'Cressida, my dear, I have an exquisite meal—jellied consommé, smoked salmon, roast duckling—which I insist on your sharing with me. I want to hear all about your day. Isn't Mr. Mullins a poppet?' She suddenly saw Jeremy and exclaimed, 'Oh, my dear, am I interrupting something? Now there's no need for a smoke-screen.'

Cressida, flushed with heat and agitation, came out of the kitchen. 'I've just succeeded in badly burning my fish, so I'd be delighted to share your meal. It's so kind of you.'

'Not in the least. Jeremy, I'm afraid you're not invited.' Arabia flicked a lace handkerchief at Jeremy in rejection. 'We're going to spend the evening talking about my darling Lucy, and I know that only bores you. I quite understand that it should. The sheik was like that, too. Men are quite unsentimental. Did I tell you about the sheik, Cressida? Ah, he was a vulture, with the heart of a lamb. His eyes, so flashing and fierce, his hooked nose, his imperious chin, and yet his heart—it was so soft he could refuse me nothing. Oh, and my husband, too, of course. We were his guests.' Arabia gave the smile that transformed her craggy face. 'I have a great many reminiscences. I shall bore you to death.'

'Not at all,' said Cressida, fascinated.

'Then come along. We'll eat first, and then

talk.'

After the meal, which was eaten by candlelight, off exquisite china, and with fine period silver, the clutter of the crowded room as a dreamlike background, Arabia relaxed on the couch among the numerous coloured cushions. She lit a cigarette and smoked it in a long jewelled holder. The rubies glowed like ripe plums on her fingers, and the tiara, crooked as usual, had the frosty sparkle of winter stars. On the back of the couch, his head tucked in his wing, Ahmed perched. The shaded lights caught glints of copper and bronze in the dim room. Miss Glory removed the dishes, and Cressida, on a low stool at Arabia's feet, listened to the vital voice above her, low and musical and dreamy now as she spoke of far-off days.

'This is the time when Lucy would come in to say good-night to me. She would be going to a ball or a party, and she would stand there shining, and so young. She would tell me not to stay awake for her, but of course I always did. I would lie listening...'

And now Lucy was listening to them talking about her. Why did Cressida suddenly have that uncanny feeling? She fancied she could hear the soft footsteps, the stealthy swish of a silk dress at the door.

'Red roses were her favourite flowers,' Arabia continued dreamily. 'She almost always wore them. I put some in her hands at the end...'

'There's someone at the door!' Cressida cried nervously.

Arabia started up. 'I didn't hear anything. Go and see who it is.'

67

Cressida went quickly, but she knew almost at once that there would be no one there. Nor was there, except, round the curve of the stairs, Dawson blundering up on his too-large feet carrying a basket of vegetables. He gave his sideways look at her.

'I've brought the shopping up,' he said humbly.

Arabia called impatiently, 'Put it in the kitchen, boy. I can't stop to talk to you tonight. I have a guest.'

Dawson obediently disappeared into the kitchen, and then clattered off downstairs.

Arabia sighed. 'That was a mistake I made,' she confessed, 'letting that dreary little woman and her son come here. I like amusing people. But she caught me at a time when I was feeling soft-hearted. She has this bad throat, and she's a widow. The boy's brilliant, they say. Well he may be, with those looks. One has to have some compensations. Come and sit down again, dear. What were we saying before Dawson interrupted us?'

'About the red roses,' Cressida said. Suddenly she couldn't sit down again. She wandered about, taut and restless.

'Yes,' Arabia murmured. 'People to amuse me, or people to love me. That is what I expect out of life.'

'Arabia, where is Lucy's grave?'

The question fell into a suddenly still room.

Then Arabia said in the harsh voice with which she had spoken to Dawson, 'Why do you ask that?'

'Because I'd like to go and see it.' Cressida regretted her question. She had not expected it to

68

distress Arabia so much. Did the old lady, with her make-believe of the room waiting for an occupant, shut out of her mind the fact that there was a grave?

Arabia suddenly began to pace up and down the room, wringing her hands. With her long brocade dress, slightly tarnished and a little grubby, and the rakish tiara, she looked like a slightly tipsy Lady Macbeth. But Lady Macbeth suggested guilt—it could not be guilt that made Arabia wring her hands and turned her face gaunt and ugly.

'You shouldn't have asked that question,' she said at last, harshly. 'It distresses me too much. You see, I could not bear to think of Lucy buried. So sweet and young. In the cold earth. Oh, no! So I had her cremated, and her ashes'—Arabia gave a harsh deep sob—'flung on the four winds. Her room upstairs, fresh with flowers—'

'Is really her grave,' Cressida whispered.

Arabia flung round. 'Do not use that word child! I cannot endure it. Oh, dear, why have we got so melancholy. Ahmed! Come here! Amuse me!' With a swift movement, she seized the sleeping parrot and flung it on to the cage of the stuffed one.

Ahmed immediately responded by squawking loudly and attacking the thin bars of the cage. Arabia, laughing now, urged him on.

'Go on! Get him! Wring his scruffy neck! Toss him on the floor! Get your claws into him!'

The pandemonium went on for several minutes, Ahmed biting at the cage bars with his vicious beak, giving his deafening squawks, and Arabia flapping her hands and shrieking with laughter. Then all at once Ahmed clambered on to the top of the cage, and subsided into his ruffled feathers. Arabia sighed deeply and straightened her tiara which had threatened to come completely adrift.

'That was amusing,' she said to Cressida, with her brilliant illuminating smile. 'I adore noise. It reminds one that one is alive. It's wonderful to be alive, isn't it?'

'I—I think I must go now,' Cressida said.

'Oh, must you my dear? I suppose you're tired after your long day. Thank you for an enchanting evening.' She took Cressida's hand in her own and began stroking it lightly. 'You must come again very soon and we won't speak of grief at all, we'll have music, and laughter. I know what we will do. We'll have a party, a house-warming for you. Mr. Moretti—can you endure his white eyebrows, my dear, like caterpillars—shall play the violin, and we may even entice Miss Glory to perform on the piano. And we'll have some good food and wine—ah, that will be gay!' The old fingers moved on the palm of Cressida's hand with their cool, dry touch. 'You're so like her, my dear, it's unbelievable.'

Impulsively Cressida leaned forward to kiss Arabia's cheek.

'It would be nice to be gay,' she said.

Downstairs, in the haven of her own room, she regretted a little that she had not asked Arabia the reason for her macabre joke of the previous evening. (Had she been locked in Lucy's room because the old lady had determined, in her obsessed mind, to get an occupant for it?) But a question such as that would probably have provoked an even more agitated outburst from Arabia, so perhaps it was best to pretend the thing had never happened. Arabia would answer a question just as it suited her to do, that was obvious. No Monty, she had said. But there had been a Monty, someone who did not fit into the pattern of Lucy's gay innocent life.

Arabia was a devious old woman, but she was also kind and immensely lovable and very lonely. Cressida was not now without qualms as to the situation in which she was finding herself, but her ready sympathy and affection was all for Arabia. She had no intention of letting her slight, never-quite-quelled, undercurrent of apprehension drive her from Dragon House. Indeed, she could not have gone, for, more even than Arabia, Lucy was holding her. She had to look at that diary again, study every entry, find out what had led to Lucy's death. It was almost as if Lucy were urging her to do this—was it to right some wrong?

Although it was late Cressida sat down to make notes.

'No Monty,' she wrote. 'Only Larry, and other obviously harmless friends. Was Monty undesirable, a fortune-hunter or a ne'er-do-well, or just socially inferior? Did he ever send Lucy red roses? (N.B. Must look in Lucy's room for old snapshots, etc. Perhaps old letters—everything of hers was untouched, Arabia said.)

'No grave,' she went on. 'Why was Arabia so distressed when I asked—'

Abruptly Cressida stopped and the pen fell from her hand as a shriek sounded upstairs.

It was a high involuntary scream, and instantly

71

suppressed. A moment later there were running footsteps. They seemed to come down the stairs. They were very soft, as if someone were in stockinged feet.

After a moment of petrified terror Cressida pulled herself together. Someone was in trouble. She had to go and see who it was.

She was almost sure the scream had come from the rooms where Mrs. Stanhope and Dawson lived. Out in the hall she switched on all the lights she could find. Then, sure that there was no one lurking in the shadows, she ran up the stairs. At the top she had to stop to get her breath. Her heart, with haste and terror, was drumming uncontrollably.

'Don't stop to be frightened,' she admonished herself, and tapped briskly at Mrs. Stanhope's door. After a moment Dawson's voice, breaking into an unexpectedly deep note, called, 'Who's there?'

'It's me. Cressida Barclay. Is there anything wrong?'

The door opened slowly. Dawson, in his pyjamas, his short stiff hair stuck on end, stood there, blinking. He hadn't his glasses on and he looked suddenly childlike and scared.

'I thought I heard someone scream,' Cressida said. 'I had to come up. Is your mother all right?'

Dawson looked shame-faced. 'It was me,' he said. 'Ma had a nightmare about that girl who was strangled, and she came in and woke me up. I felt her hand on my face, and I yelled.'

Mrs. Stanhope, bundled into a wool dressing-gown, that almost obscured her so that one could see only the large glasses and her thin

72

pointed nose, was suddenly there, saying in her apologetic gasping voice, 'I'm so sorry we frightened you, Miss Barclay. I had a bad dream.'

'You shouldn't have come in like that without making a sound,' Dawson complained. 'It was me that got the fright.'

'That poor girl was on my mind,' Mrs. Stanhope whispered.

'I'm sorry I disturbed you,' Cressida apologised. 'I guess I was uneasy, too, and when I heard the scream—'

'It happened so near here,' whispered Mrs. Stanhope. 'You must let Dawson call for you at nights, Miss Barclay.'

'That's very kind of you to suggest it, Mrs. Stanhope. But I'll be all right. Really. Now you go back to bed and get some sleep. And didn't your doctor say you shouldn't talk so much?'

Mrs. Stanhope busily took her pad from her pocket, and wrote, 'She was wearing a red rose.'

A ripple of fear went through Cressida. Red roses again. But a dead girl wearing a red rose could have no possible connection with Dragon House and a frightened little woman having a nightmare. They were just a recurring and slightly sinister theme.

'I'd give your mother a couple of aspirins,' Cressida said to Dawson.

He nodded importantly. 'I have something more effective than aspirins. Come on, Ma, go back to bed.'

Mrs. Stanhope nodded meekly. The high collar of her dressing-gown, which she had clutched closely round her, slipped a little as she returned the writing pad to her pocket, and Cressida

73

caught a glimpse of the mark on her cheek.

'Why, you're hurt!' she exclaimed.

Dawson giggled. 'She bumped into the door on her way in to me. Drunk, that's what she was. Weren't you, Ma?'

With which bizarre humour he bundled his mother back into the room. Cressida turned slowly away, remembering the soft footsteps she had heard. They could have been Mrs. Stanhope's, who, on bare feet, had run blindly in the dark into her son's room. Or they could have been those of an intruder who had struck Mrs. Stanhope and made Dawson scream.

No, that was an unlikely explanation. For why should the two conceal so frightening a happening? They must be telling the truth.

But as she reached her own room once more Cressida had a peculiar thought. Dawson's voice now had the depth of a man's. It only occasionally wobbled into falsetto. Could he have screamed on so high a note? And why had he looked so scared?

CHAPTER SEVEN

When Cressida had gone Arabia suddenly could not bear to be alone. She put her finger on the bell and held it there until Miss Glory came panting up the stairs.

'For Lord's sake, what now, madam?' Miss Glory stood flat and uncompromising in the doorway.

'Are you having an affair with Moretti?' Arabia dropped the question with complete aplomb.

74

'Madam!' Miss Glory was suddenly seven feet tall, standing there rigid with outrage.

'Oh, too bad!' Arabia sighed. 'It would have been diverting. For me as well as you. Life can be so deadly dull.'

'It isn't dull for you now, madam. You've got the girl.'

'What do you know about that?' Arabia demanded icily.

'Well, I know you're trying to do something unhealthy. Bringing back the dead might be one way of making life less dull, but, if I may say so, it isn't fair to that nice young girl.'

'And why isn't it fair to her? She has a good flat, very cheap, she likes me—I know that, because she is naturally honest and easy to read—and I promise you she shall not suffer.'

'How can you promise that?' Miss Glory muttered. 'She'll have her head turned. She has to go home to her boy-friend in the country some time. How can she do that if you've pampered her too much here?'

'You forget, Miss Glory, that she may not be the type to live happily in the country with a dull young man. In fact, I am sure she isn't. Apart from anything else, look at the future unhappiness I may be saving her.'

'Madam, you wouldn't come between man and wife!'

'Wait until they are man and wife, Miss Glory. And speaking of that,' Arabia's dark, liquid eyes were full of pleasurable malice, 'if you are not having an affair with Moretti, have you asked him his intentions?'

Miss Glory tossed her head and sniffed loudly.

75

She did not deign to answer.

'Although he's the sort I'd imagine to have a wife somewhere. Probably deserted, poor thing.'

'Madam, you must excuse me, but I can't stand here listening to that sort of talk.'

Arabia gave her rich chuckle.

'Sorry, Miss Glory. I'm teasing you. Your Moretti is amusing, and any sin can be forgiven for that. But I don't think you ought to trust him too far.'

'Who's talking about trusting anybody?' Miss Glory had relaxed enough to converse again, although her voice was still prickly with offence. 'Of course I don't trust Moretti. A violinist in a night-club, and with all those pretty girls—though what they look like by daylight is another thing. I can be seen first thing in the morning, unprinked, and little do I care. He knows where he is with me.'

'Yes. Go on,' urged Arabia, full of interest.

Miss Glory realised she was committing herself farther than she had meant to. She took refuge in dignity once more.

'If you just had me up here to talk about Moretti, madam, I'll ask to be excused.'

'No, no, don't go, Miss Glory. I want to talk about a party I'm going to have for Cressida. A house-warming.'

'What, just us ones in the house, madam?'

'Why not? This is where she belongs. Plenty of good food and wine and music. I want you to ask Moretti to play, and of course yourself—'

'I expect you're hinting that I'll be more use in the kitchen.'

'Well, I must admit you cook duckling in the
76

most delectable way. That sauce tonight, and the cold consommé, and the delicious strawberry mousse—'

'Thank you, madam,' Miss Glory said with dignity. Suddenly she relaxed and her thin face creased in a triumphant smile. 'I'd like to see those night-club girls roast a duckling like that. When are you planning to have the party, madam?'

'I think on Thursday evening.'

'Then, if you'll excuse me, I've got plenty of time to work out the menu without doing so at this hour.'

'No, don't go!' Arabia cried suddenly, in a pleading voice.

'Is there something the matter, madam?'

'No, nothing.' Arabia pressed her hands to her breast. She said, almost in a whisper. 'Tonight I am afraid of old sins.'

Miss Glory snorted. 'Oh, you're play-acting again!'

'I never play-act!' Arabia rose magnificently. 'Every moment of my life is lived! Every beat of my heart brings me some emotion—sorrow, happiness, amusement, scorn...'

'And what, may I ask, are you feeling at this moment?'

Arabia lifted her heavy-lidded eyes. 'Fear!' she whispered.

'Ho! That's your bad conscience, I don't doubt. You can't ask anyone to live with that for you, madam. So I'll be off to my bed.'

And with that Miss Glory did go, clattering on her long flat feet, leaving Arabia in the shadowy room, with even Ahmed, his head tucked in his

77

feathers, sound asleep.

At first the old lady made a great show of plumping out cushions, straightening furniture, emptying ash-trays. But at last there was nothing left to do. There was only her bed to which to go. And as soon as she lay down in the dark and closed her eyes the voice would come to her.

She had been so sure that the presence of Cressida, young and gay and light-hearted, would dispel it, send it back to the shadows to which it belonged.

But this had not happened. Last night the hissed 'I hate you!' had been more virulent than ever. Finally she had taken two sleeping tablets.

Tonight, however, she would not need to take any. She was too tired. She was almost asleep already. It had been a long day, with the pleasurable excitement of having Cressida—the pretty creature—to dinner to wind it up. She would think all the time of Cressida, with her lively face, and warm soft hands, and keep ghosts away.

She undressed quickly, putting on her elaborate silk nightgown and over it a light frilly bedjacket, and climbed into the big bed. She was so tired she even forgot to set Ahmed, as a pale-grey guardian, on the bedpost. He would find his way there in the morning and wake her. She needed no guardian tonight. She was too tired...

And Lucy did not speak to her in that hating voice. She screamed instead. A high, far-off scream that scarcely aroused Arabia from her sleep...

CHAPTER EIGHT

In the morning there was the expected letter from Tom.

Cressida opened it in some trepidation. It began, 'Dear Cressida', so she knew at once that he was still in his chilly, offended mood, otherwise it would have been 'Darling Cress' or just 'Darling'.

However, beyond a reproval for her continued stubborn behaviour, he was friendly enough, and full of good sense. He warned Cressida about allowing Arabia to get too possessive, as it would be embarrassing to find oneself an heiress, and then have the family turn up and make a scandal. Besides, as Cressida knew, by 1957 he would be making sufficient to keep her very comfortably.

He added that Miss Madden didn't care about being in the house alone, and to see that Cressida didn't lose a good tenant he had felt bound to keep her company now and again.

But he was human enough, at the end of the letter, to admit that he missed her.

Tom, Cressida thought fairly, was really being very sweet. She was well aware of the effort it must have cost him to write that letter. He had had to bring himself to admit her right to independence, and to be as generous about it as one could expect under the circumstances. Tom hated to admit he was ever wrong about anything, and to give him his due he seldom was wrong. The fact that he was allowing her this victory proved that he must love her very much. Even what he said about Arabia and Lucy was probably true, and it was certainly true that she suffered from too vivid an imagination.

But all that had happened was not imagination. There was the locked door, and the macabre joke of the key and the note on her table, there was Arabia's distress last night when she had talked of Lucy's grave, and last of all there was the scream that had reputedly come from the usually self-possessed Dawson.

Cressida was deeply pondering those things when Miss Glory came in with the morning tea.

'I might as well make a habit of this,' she said in her uncompromising way. 'I'm making it for myself, and it's no trouble to bring you a cup.'

'That's awfully kind of you,' Cressida said gratefully. Miss Glory was a study in brown today, from the faded colour of her hair to her pale-beige skin, the chocolate-coloured dress, and the long narrow shoes. As she seldom smiled, she was not exactly a cheerful sight, but one suspected that her kindness was completely sincere.

'What did you do to upset Mrs. Bolton last night?' she went on.

'Why, nothing. Was she upset?'

'She was in one of her moods. She likes to bait people then. Oh, well, I'm used to it. Expect I'd miss it if it didn't happen.'

'I only mentioned Lucy's grave,' Cressida said tentatively. 'She said there wasn't one.'

Miss Glory gaped suddenly. 'Not a grave! But of course there must be. Well, I mean to say! The body wasn't spirited away, was it?'

'It was cremated.'

80

Miss Glory's long hands flapped. Her face was completely sceptical.

'You can't tell me that, my dear. Haven't you ever heard Mrs. Bolton on that subject? She can't abide cremation. She's got her three husbands buried in large mausoleums all in different cemeteries, to save hurting their feelings, poor dears, and she visits them all turn and turn about. No, my dear, she hasn't told you the truth.'

Miss Glory was suddenly reflective. 'Now why should she mislead you like that? Oh, well, it's just her way of amusing herself, I expect. She so loves to do the unexpected. She should have been on the stage. All that talent wasted.'

Miss Glory, who knew Arabia a great deal better than Cressida did, was quite satisfied with that explanation, and prepared to depart. But Cressida suddenly called her back.

'Miss Glory, do you think it's because something peculiar happened to Lucy?'

'What sort of peculiar do you mean, dear? There's plenty can happen to a girl.'

'I don't mean that sort of thing. I mean'—Cressida's voice was only a whisper—'murder.'

After a moment of gaping Miss Glory threw back her head and gave a hoot of laughter.

'What! You mean Mrs. Bolton's little precious! But the murderer would have had to get past Mama—and, pray, how would he do that? Now you pay attention to me, Miss Barclay, and don't let that old woman and her past get on your mind too much. She loves to build up atmosphere, whether it's about her pet sheik or her camels and vultures, or just about that morbid room she

81

keeps upstairs pretending that some day someone will come back to it. You take what she says with a grain of salt. Why, if you were to meet Lucy now you'd probably find she was just an ordinary person, not even particularly pretty.'

'Perhaps you're right,' Cressida agreed. But she knew quite surely inside herself that Miss Glory was not right. Lucy had not been an ordinary person. She had been, like her mother, full of personality and charm. She may have been headstrong, she may even have had intrigues which she had carefully concealed from her mother. But she had lived very deeply and emotionally in this house, and for some reason, probably a desperately unhappy one, Arabia denied her a grave.

At work that morning Mr. Mullins looked at her with his bright kind eyes and said, 'You didn't sleep well, Miss Barclay?'

'Yes, I did,' Cressida lied.

'Has Arabia been keeping you up late with her stories?'

'Stories?'

'She has a remarkable imagination, that lady.'

Mr. Mullins's hair shone like thistledown. His eyes were gentle and innocent. Cressida said impulsively,

'Mr. Mullins, if someone who was dead hadn't got a grave, what would the reason be?'

Mr. Mullins pondered. 'It could be that the ashes were scattered, or it could be—'

'Yes?' Cressida said breathlessly.

'That the body wasn't recoverable. But why this morbid subject, Miss Barclay? Now I want you to serve customers today, so don't get yourself too

82

dusty. Though you might just clean this candelabra. I've a customer coming to look at it. It came from Arabia, you know. The stuff that woman has had in the past. That rolltop desk, too. It belonged to her late husband, I believe. It's stuffed full of junk. I've never had time to go through it. Of course it could be that the body in question wasn't even dead, eh?'

That was when Cressida got the idea to go to the local public library and search the files of old newspapers. She skipped lunch in order to do this. Arabia had said Lucy had died nineteen years ago, so she knew pretty certainly the year. It was only a matter of skimming through the files of newspapers for that year. She might not be able to do the whole year in one hour. If not, she could come back tomorrow and finish.

The files were down in the basement, the girl at the library told her. She found that she was not the only one in that large chilly room, with its smell of musty paper. There were several elderly gentlemen, and one girl with dragged-back hair and glasses. There was no sound except the occasional rustle of paper. Cressida chose *The Times* as that being surely the paper in which Lucy's death notice would appear, and skimmed through the 'Bs'. Borling, Borne, Botting, Bolton ... In every fourth or fifth paper there was a death of a Bolton. Husband of, wife of, darling granny to, relict of ... But no 'Beloved daughter of Arabia Bolton'.

The print danced in front of Cressida's eyes. She began to feel gloomy and depressed. Lucy had no grave, but this cold stone-floored room that never echoed to the sound of voices was like a grave.

Bolling, Box, Bonnington...

'I told you I didn't want a half-starved model,' came a sibilant whisper in her ear.

Cressida suppressed a startled scream. She turned to see the inevitable Jeremy Winter. He had this way of materialising as silently as his cat, Mimosa. His hair was brushed smoothly today, his face seemed leaner than ever, and his eyes more alert and sparkling.

'Do you follow me?' Cressida whispered angrily.

'Actually I do. I came to take you to lunch, and just saw you whisking round the corner. When you came in here I told myself you were in search of culture so I couldn't disturb you. I gave you half an hour, which is all one should spend on culture at lunch-time. But I find that isn't what you're seeking after all.'

His eyes slipped over the open newspaper. Cressida's hand went instinctively over the column she had been reading, but she could not hope to deceive those alert eyes.

'That's a morbid thing to be doing,' he said gently.

'I have to find our about her! I have to.'

'Do you think she isn't dead?'

'If she hasn't got a grave, how can she be?'

'Arabia might not have told you the truth about that. There might be a reason why she doesn't want you to see the grave.'

'She was so distressed,' Cressida said, remembering Arabia's sudden violent upheaval of the room, with Ahmed shrieking, and cushions tumbling on the floor.

84

'In any case,' Jeremy's reasonable voice went on, 'this is a very long and tortuous way of finding anything out. Why not get a death certificate?'

'Of course!'

'In fact, if you'll lunch with me now I may even do that for you.'

'Oh, would you?'

'Not that I'm in the least suspicious, but there are one or two things—Well, never mind now. Come and eat.'

They went into a near-by café. Emerging from the gloom of the basement, Cressida's spirits returned with a rush and she was prepared to be pleasant even to the impudent Mr. Winter.

'And how's Tom?' he asked, when he had given their order to the waitress.

Cressida looked up sharply. 'How did you know I had a letter from Tom?'

'I didn't know. But I thought you would have, Tom being Tom.'

Cressida was going to hotly defend Tom, then suddenly she found herself laughing, with tenderness for the absent Tom.

'You're so right. He is Tom. He's forgiven me already, although I know he's terribly hurt. He worries about what people think. And he's afraid already that I'll get involved in lawsuits with Arabia's family.'

'As you well may do.'

'What do you mean?'

'Arabia may play-act a lot, but she's a woman of violent emotions. I thought your intelligence would have told you that already.'

Cressida watched him warily.

'If she grows fond enough of you—and she's

85

going to, that's obvious—you may find yourself an heiress.'

'Oh, I'd give all the money away to an orphans' home,' Cressida said blithely.

'For heaven's sake, be realistic! What sort of a world do you live in?'

'I just can't visualise such an unlikely thing happening,' Cressida confessed. 'And if Arabia did suddenly, for some fantastic reason, say that she wanted to leave me some money, I'd have to accept so as not to hurt her feelings—she's terribly sensitive, you know—but honestly I would give it all away. I wouldn't want it myself.'

'Eat some food,' Jeremy said briefly, 'and just come back and live in this world with us. The one you're in, where you receive large fortunes from strange old women and then toss them away like autumn leaves, may be pleasant, but it isn't practicable. There'd bound to be long-lost relations come along, as Tom points out, and make all sorts of unpleasantness.'

'Oh, don't be absurd.' Cressida was quite undisturbed. 'It's you who are living in a fictitious world. Those things only happen in books. I'm just a working girl, and I'm going to write a book, and I like living in Dragon House for that purpose, and I like being kind to Arabia because she's terribly sweet and kind, and also very lonely. Am I to refuse to speak to her just because of the remote possibility of getting this fortune, which probably doesn't exist, anyway? She can't be rich or she wouldn't sell things to Mr. Mullins. And, anyway ...' Cressida paused a minute before she said under her breath, 'Lucy won't let me go. I have to find out about Lucy.

86

'And another thing,' she went on vigorously, for Jeremy's head was bent, he had a pencil in his hand, and he did not appear to be listening to her, 'Tom says if you insist on drawing me I should expect to get a fee for it.'

Jeremy gave a sudden shout of laughter. His face creased into deep lines, and his eyes shone.

'Good old Tom. Salt of the earth. Name your fee, my dear child. But in the meantime, do sit still.'

Cressida looked across the table. She saw that Jeremy was rapidly sketching her on the back of the menu.

'I can't resist it,' he said, without looking up. 'I'm in love with your face. It's like suddenly waking up to a spring day after ice and snow. It's like finding the first daffodil. Please sit still. It isn't late yet, and Mr. Mullins knows it's me you're out with. Of course I'll pay you a fee, my darling Cressida. You have the most paintable face. I'm doing an illustration for a short story. It's by a very famous writer who demands the best. He'd adore you, but I'll never let him set eyes on you or I'll lose you. The story is called "Death is a Red Rose".'

That was the moment when Jeremy Winter stopped being a harmless, amusing, and always slightly impudent friend and became a stranger.

What did she know of him, after all? He lived in Dragon House, mysteriously in the basement. He had carried her in the other day, almost as if she were a fish caught in his net. He laughed at her and persistently made sketches of her and pretended to be engaged in currently saving her life. He gave her advice that seemed sincere. She thought he was a friend. And then suddenly he made a double-edged remark that could mean nothing or a good deal.

Did he know that Lucy's favourite flowers had been red roses? Did he know that they were always sent to her before a ball or a party, and that she had been buried with a cluster of them in her hands? (Buried? But where was her grave?)

Did he know that already red roses suggested death to Cressida, and that now he had put her inner, strange, cold fear into words? Had he done it deliberately, or had that been a purely chance remark? He insisted afterwards that it was. He offered to show Cressida the manuscript with the title on it. His remark probably was quite innocent, but it gave Cressida a haunting dread that she could not dispel all day.

She went home that night resolved to spend another evening in Lucy's quiet empty room sifting through the relics left there: the clothes, the silk stockings and dancing shoes, the girlish jewellery, the old snapshots and the diary. Surely she could remove this persistent feeling that it was by no ordinary means that Lucy had met her death—if she had met it at all.

It was true, as she had told Jeremy, that Lucy would not let her leave Dragon House. She had this extraordinary urge to seek out the whole of Lucy's story. She was convinced now that Arabia was only telling her part of it, probably all that she knew. But a great deal had gone on in Lucy's mind and perhaps in happenings concealed from her mother. And the strangest thing of all was that although it was now a long time ago, a quarter of a lifetime, it seemed as if it had been only yesterday. The house was still permeated with the tension that must have filled it during the last days of Lucy's short life. That feeling was unexplainable, but everyone in the house had it, Cressida knew.

There was Mrs. Stanhope with her nervous jumpiness, Dawson with his mind morbidly fixed on murders, Mr. Moretti playing his persistently macabre music, Miss Glory too determinedly practical, Jeremy making his subtle double-edged remarks. And, most of all, Arabia, full of melodrama and exhibitionism, as if she were afraid to be quiet; as if something or someone would speak to her in the silence and what she heard would be unbearable.

Even Mr. Mullins, who did not live in Dragon House, had caught its peculiar tension, and spoke his gentle words of warning.

Yet that evening no one could have said there was any tension at all. The house was as quiet and well-bred as its exterior promised. Dawson tapped politely at Cressida's door and proffered her the bread and vegetables he had bought for her on the way home.

'No more news about that murder. The police don't find out much,' he said in a conversational voice, as if he were discussing the price of cabbages. He said his mother was well, and they both apologised for disturbing Cressida last night.

Cressida said lightly, 'I may be disturbing you tonight, because I'm going up to Lucy's room to work.'

'You're writing her story?' Dawson said admiringly. 'I'll tell Ma.'

Later, Cressida, thinking that if everyone knew

she were there no one would dare to play tricks on her, told Arabia also that she was going to be upstairs. Arabia gave a tremendous sigh, and nodded her head understandingly.

'Don't let Lucy make you too sad, my dear. I've had enough sadness to pay for all my sins, but you're too young to suffer.'

'Your sins?' Cressida queried.

Arabia had a flash of her colourful melodrama.

'Of course I've sinned. Gloriously. Fine big shocking sins. Never mean sordid ones. I remember that night in Khartoum—no, never mind now, your ears are too young and pretty.' She leaned forward to pat Cressida's cheek. 'I wasn't bad, dear, only high-spirited. Oh, a little bad, too.' She gave her ravishing smile, her tired old eyes suddenly glowing with unquenchable life. 'They would all fall in love with me, you know. It was quite embarrassing and inconvenient at times. You will find the same thing happen to you, now you've escaped from your watchdog in the country.'

'Did Lucy?' Cressida asked involuntarily.

Age fell over Arabia's face like a mask. The light in her eyes died.

'My darling little girl didn't live long enough. But they would have. Yes, they would have. Now run along and look at her things. They'll talk to you better than I can.'

Miss Glory had overheard her conversation with Arabia, because she slid past them on the stairs, her long face contorted in a meaningful wink. Jeremy had known at lunchtime of her intentions. There was only Mr. Moretti left, and he didn't really matter because he would be away at his night-club. As it happened, Cressida met him in the hall just as he was leaving.

It was the first time she had met him since their preliminary introduction.

He was dressed in evening clothes, and looked plump and dapper. But with his pale eyes, his thick light eyebrows and lashes, he had a curiously faceless look. His teeth, too, were very small so that when he smiled his mouth made a dark cavern. He was almost comical, and certainly not the kind of man who would cause tremors in any feminine breast other than Miss Glory's flat ardent one. Except for his voice. One had to make that exception, for it was oddly pleasant and persuasive.

Now he said, 'Good evening, Miss Barclay. Please tell me at once if my violin disturbs you.'

'It really doesn't, Mr. Moretti. I'm out all day and you're out all night, almost. Only I wonder why you have a taste for such sad music.'

'Ah, yes, indeed. I'm afraid that's a natural reaction after playing dance music all night. From the rumba to the requiem. That's how it is.'

He gave his wide, dark-mouthed smile, his thick lashes hiding his eyes. He bowed gallantly, and was gone. He's just like something kept in a dark room and gone pallid, Cressida was thinking, when she realised that Miss Glory was watching her from the end of the hall.

Miss Glory was in love with that poor little unnatural product of night life, she realised. Suddenly she was both sorry and sympathetic and envious. It must be wonderful to be in love with someone like that, so that you got infinite pleasure out of every glimpse of him, out of every nuance of his voice. And it didn't matter whether he looked like a king or a caterpillar. At the same moment she knew that she was not really in love with Tom. Standing there in Arabia's marble-floored hall she knew drearily that she had never been in love nor known its glory and despair.

How could she write Lucy's story, which she knew instinctively was one of deep romantic love, when she had never been in love herself?

Absorbed in this sudden disturbing revelation, Cressida did not remember Mr. Moretti's words until she was in Lucy's room, and looking with her now familiar distaste at the waiting bed, the fresh flowers, the carefully-laid-out night-gown. From the rumba to the requiem, he had said.

And he had been talking of Lucy. Of that she was convinced.

Had it been a chance remark, cleverly significant but meaning nothing more than its aptness? Or had he some personal knowledge of Lucy? Did he know how her little feet, scarcely stopped dancing, had come to their premature quiescence?

It had been a very short illness, Arabia had said.

What doctor had Lucy had, what minister summoned hastily to her bedside, what gravedigger, what grave?

Cressida turned to pick up the innocent and unrevealing diary. Suddenly she looked more closely at it. Why, a number of pages had been removed from the middle of it. The date on which the last entry had been made was the third of April, and the next page showed the tenth of July. Three whole months were missing. What had happened in those months? What revealing entries had Lucy made that someone had considered better destroyed?

Cressida, trembling with excitement, was going to rush down to Arabia. But suddenly she paused. She could already visualise the hooded look coming over Arabia's eyes, she could hear the haughty old voice saying, 'And why, pray, should I destroy anything my darling child wrote? Those are the blank days after her death that I couldn't bear to live through. So I destroyed the empty pages.' She knew with certainly that Arabia would make some explanation like that, just as she denied the existence of Lucy's grave.

Three months of missing pages and a missing grave. Now her instinct that here was an absorbing story was proving correct. In a fever of excitement Cressida began opening drawers, unfolding gloves, stockings, handkerchiefs, silk underwear. Momentarily she forgot that they belonged to a dead girl. Somewhere here among Lucy's things there must be more clues to those lost months.

The sweet heavy scent of dried roses filled the room. The house was utterly still. Then, slipped down at the back of the bottom drawer, she found the letter.

It wasn't a letter at all. It was just a beginning. It said, 'Darling, darling, darling ...' and then there was no more.

Cressida groped feverishly in the gap at the back of the drawer. Her fingers touched on something soft. She drew it out. It was a hand-knitted baby's glove.

She couldn't stay up there alone. Suddenly the

93

room was uncanny with its untold story. She had to know the truth. Arabia was the only person to tell it to her. Clutching the scrap of knitting she ran down the stairs and tapped on Arabia's door.

Arabia called eagerly, 'Is that you, Cressida? I'm in bed, but do come in, my darling, and kiss me goodnight. It's so kind of you to think of an old lady.'

Sitting up in the big four-poster, Arabia had lost her majestic posture and looked much more frail and defenceless. The bones protruded at the base of her neck, her thin wrists emerged fragilely from the cuffs of her woolly bed jacket. Now she looked mortal indeed, and no longer indestructible. Even her smile glimmered in a childlike way as she lifted her face to be kissed.

Was she really as gentle and helpless as this, Cressida wondered, or was she just a consummate actress?

'That's what Lucy used to do,' she said in her soft satisfied voice. 'She would creep in to see if I were awake when she came home at night, and if I were she'd stop and talk about the ball and the people. Just here, she would sit.' Arabia patted the side of the bed invitingly. 'She never looked tired, always so fresh and sparkling. She was one of those people on whom a dress never crushed, or flowers never died.'

In fact, thought Cressida with sudden bleak conviction, she was a dream creature who with her death had become invested with an impossibly angelic purity. She clutched the baby's glove, and felt like an assassin.

'I found things in Lucy's room tonight,' she said.

'You did?' Was Arabia's attention suddenly more than a smiling politeness? 'But of course you would. Those darling relics—'

'This,' said Cressida flatly, holding up the ridiculously miniature garment.

'But—why, it's a baby's glove!'

The heavy lids dropped abruptly over the suddenly aware eyes. The old face was closed. It was all ridges and shadows, a sculptured face telling nothing.

'Lucy must have been knitting it for one of her friends.' Arabia's voice was too glib. 'She knitted very well. I used to wonder where she got her talent. Me, I couldn't—'

Cressida cut into the half-finished sentence.

'Arabia, why do you lie to me? You've been very kind and sweet and I do appreciate that, but I don't appreciate being lied to when there's absolutely no need. Lucy should be nothing to me, a girl I never knew, and dead nearly twenty years. It shouldn't matter to me if this glove was being knitted for her own baby or not. But you liken me to Lucy all the time, and therefore I must know the truth. It makes me feel foolish not to, and I waste my sympathies.'

The hooded lids were raised now, the eyes dark and shocked. There was no doubt whatever about their shock. In that minute Arabia had changed from her rôle of a sad resigned mother to that of a frightened old woman.

'This was for Lucy's own baby, wasn't it?' Cressida insisted.

'I—don't know.'

Cressida began to lose her patience. Ever since finding the glove and that beginning of a letter

95

that was also, somehow, a cry for help, she had been conscious of an almost unbearable tension. Why didn't people tell her the truth? It was imperative that she should know it, and this not from curiosity but because Arabia had invested her with the dead Lucy's rôle, and she had to know what it had been. She could not endure a lie.

'Arabia!' She tried to speak gently. 'You must know. Lucy was your own daughter. You loved her. You must know whether or not she was going to have a baby.'

'Oh, no, no!' Arabia burst out harshly.

Instinctively Cressida knew that in that moment Arabia was not speaking to her but to some torturing image in her own mind. But now at least she was no longer acting, so there might be a chance of getting the truth. Momentarily without remorse, Cressida pursued her questioning.

'Arabia, is Lucy really dead?'

Then Arabia came to life. She jerked upright, her eyes blazing, her face rigid with suffering.

'Dead! Of course she's dead. How dare you suggest I would lie about the greatest grief in my life! How dare you!' Then the rigidity went out of the old lady's face and she sank back against the pillows. Her mouth trembled. 'Forgive me, my dear. You young people—so honest—so ruthless ... And yet you're gentle and pretty, like Lucy. I was pretending you were Lucy back...'

Now she was acting again, Cressida knew. Yet she had the strange feeling that she was acting to hide her shock and fear.

'Arabia,' she said gently, 'did you take those three months out of Lucy's diary because you

96

didn't want any record of the baby?'

'You notice too much!' the old lady muttered.

'It was because Lucy was not married? But wouldn't Larry have married her? Or wasn't it'—Cressida had a sudden illumination—'wasn't it Larry's baby?'

'He needn't have known about it,' Arabia muttered. 'If my plan had worked—' She began to twist her hands together in acute distress. Tears gathered in her brilliant eyes. 'It was all my fault,' she said. 'I persuaded her to take the risk. I'—her voice rose to that of a tragedienne—'I killed her!'

It made Lucy's charming room, with its fresh flowers, its carefully preserved relics, a farce; but it also explained why it existed, why Arabia built up the memory of a lovely innocent young girl, and even why she had so warmly welcomed Cressida into her house. For all these years she had suffered from a dreadful and lonely guilt complex, and this was her way of expiating it. Now everything was clear.

Cressida felt nothing but pity and affection for the old woman who put so gallant a face on life, and endured her nightmares in private. She stooped and put her arms round the frail form and said gently,

'Don't be sad, Arabia dear. Don't be sad. It's all over long ago. And now I'm here. And I'm not frightened of Lucy any more.'

'So young to die,' Arabia murmured. She was relaxing already. But as she lifted her eyes, dry now and no longer evasive, Cressida had a curious feeling that her own apprehension had passed to Arabia.

CHAPTER NINE

So much was explained now. It didn't worry Cressida that Lucy's story was suddenly a little sordid. It made her a human being, and not full of that innocence and purity that had somehow haunted Cressida. Was she a little sorry that the mystery had been so easily solved, and that even Arabia's eccentricities, such as mischievously locking her in the other night so that Lucy's room should have the inmate she wanted—the young innocent pretty girl whom she had destroyed— were now understandable? She didn't think so. She still wanted to write Lucy's story, and now she had a flesh-and-blood creature as her subject.

Who was the man who had led her to this pass, the one to whom she had cried despairingly, 'Darling, darling, darling . . .'? It would be Monty, of course, whose name had been erased from her diary. Where was he now? Where was Larry, who, had Lucy recovered, was to have been deceived? What had they told him about her death?

And had Lucy wanted to have the baby? Had she begged and prayed to Arabia to be allowed to have it? The mute evidence of the knitted glove suggested this. Arabia's remorse, after Lucy's death, must have been terrible.

Cressida was full of pity for them both, the proud and lonely old woman and the dead girl.

There was still Tom's letter to be written that evening. But now it required a tremendous effort. Oakshott and the calm unexciting life there seemed so far away. Cressida began by saying the

98

encouraging things expected of her about Tom's golf handicap, and then suggested that if Mary Madden was finding it too lonely in the house certainly he must call on her occasionally. Mary was a sensible intelligent girl of whom he would thoroughly approve.

She added that she was enjoying her new job tremendously, and that Mr. Mullins was a poppet. Then suddenly she could find nothing more to say. The latest development about Lucy was not for Tom's ears. She knew at once that he would neither understand nor approve. He would say, 'She looks as if she got what was coming to her, and the old woman, too.' It wouldn't matter to him that two people had broken their hearts—Lucy over her mysterious lover, and Arabia over the death she had inadvertently brought to her treasured daughter. He would tell her impatiently that it wasn't any of her business, and it was unhealthy to get too interested in it. Perhaps he would be right.

But she had promised Arabia to stay, she wanted to stay. Besides Arabia there was Mr. Mullins and his fascinating shop, and the work that she loved, and as well—she had to admit it—the dark, thin, laughing face of Jeremy Winter kept interposing itself in front of her image of Tom. She didn't want to go home just yet; no, not just yet...

In the morning there was another letter from Tom. It reproached her for not having written again. The least she could do, he pointed out, since she persisted in her rather selfish behaviour, was to write to him each day. Things were as usual there. He had taken the liberty of calling at

Cressida's house to see if everything was in order, and Mary Madden had persuaded him to drink tea with her. She was a sensible, responsible sort of person, as well as being attractive, and at present there was nothing for Cressida to worry about.

Cressida smiled on reading this. Tom, nice simple Tom, thought he was subtly going to make her jealous by oblique references to Mary Madden's charms. He didn't know that he was doing precisely what Cressida had suggested he should. If it came to that, Mary and Tom were ideally suited. They were both pleasant and unimaginative, they did not suffer from her wild flights of fancy and her sudden loyalties and enthusiasms.

Did she mind that they would probably become very good friends? Cressida had to admit honestly that she didn't. She was remembering her sudden disturbing revelation last night when she had known certainly that she was not in love with Tom—at least not in the way that Miss Glory was so improbably with Vincent Moretti, or in the way Lucy had been with the lover to whom she had called in despair. What had happened to them? Had Arabia, in her sudden magnificent anger, forbidden him the house, or had he wilfully deserted Lucy in her trouble?

There it was again, Lucy's story nagging at her, giving her no peace. Idly she picked up the other letter that had come in the morning mail. She opened it, and then she gave a great gasp of disbelief.

Printed across the sheet of paper was the draft of a death notice. It read,

Barclay, Cressida Lucy. On 23rd October 1955 at Dragon House, South Kensington, in her twenty-third year. Red roses only.

Underneath this were the scrawled words, 'Is this what you were looking for?'

This was too much to tolerate. So it had been Jeremy Winter playing the tricks on her, after all. She might have known, after his unconventional behaviour that first day, that he was not to be trusted, he with his mocking eyes and air of gentle scorn. Oh, this was too much, this horrible macabre joke!

Cressida flung out of her room and hurried purposefully to the basement stairs. She almost knocked over Miss Glory, who was approaching with her morning tea-tray.

'Sorry!' she called. 'I can't stop.'

Miss Glory turned a long, mildly interested face to watch her.

'I say, Mr. Winter will hardly be up yet. Not that that would worry me, but—'

'Nor me, either,' Cressida retorted.

She reached the bottom of the stairs and banged unceremoniously at Jeremy's door. A far-off voice from within called, 'Just a moment. Coming now.'

And then Jeremy, clad in a rather gaudy silk dressing-gown, and with Mimosa in his arms, appeared at the door.

'Why, good morning,' he said with pleasure. 'Were you going to give me a sitting now? If you'd wait—ah, no, I see I'm mistaken.'

He hadn't needed to take even that long to

realise her anger. She thrust the piece of paper at him, saying icily,

'If this is your idea of a joke, it isn't mine. I am not amused. I ask you to find out about Lucy for me, and you do this—this unspeakable thing.'

'Why, what is it?' Jeremy asked, looking at the sheet of paper in bewilderment.

'And don't pretend to be shocked or surprised. You can't deceive me that way again. I'm just asking you to stop following me about and interfering in what I am doing. I never want to speak to you again.'

'But, Cressida! Listen!'

Cressida was already at the top of the stairs. The next moment she had reached her room, was inside and the door safely shut behind her. Now she couldn't hear Jeremy Winter's protests of innocence, for of course he would, as usual, deny all knowledge of this latest outrage. Now, also, she could burst into tears without his intolerably amused eyes on her.

But she was not alone, after all. Miss Glory said, 'Excuse me, Miss Barclay. I was just leaving your tea. Is anything the matter?'

Cressida made a desperate effort to control her tears. She looked wildly at Miss Glory's flat figure, thought that to lay her head on that shoulder would be equivalent to laying it on a piece of brown cardboard, and realised that she hadn't any shoulder in the whole world on which to weep.

'Nothing's wrong, really,' she managed to say. 'I expect I was suddenly a bit homesick.'

Miss Glory's eyes were sceptical.

'I might not be very bright, Miss Barclay, but

102

why rushing down to Mr. Winter's flat should suddenly make you homesick doesn't entirely make sense to me.'

'It's nothing to do with him!' Cressida denied vigorously.

But it was, of course. It was the dismal realisation that she had spurned Tom, her faithful and reliable Tom, partly because he was so stubborn and dull and predictable, but also more than a little because Jeremy's alert, restless image had come between them. And now Jeremy was not to be trusted, and pride forbade her going back to Tom—even if she had wanted to.

'Of course I'm lucky,' Miss Glory observed. 'I know when I'm in love and who I'm in love with. When the thing hits me, it hits me, and one might as well try to withstand an H-bomb. But with you I can see it's different. You don't really know your own mind.'

'I do know my own mind!' Cressida flared. 'But if someone could do a thing like that to you, could you still like them?'

She told Miss Glory what had happened, and had the doubtful satisfaction of seeing first incredulity and then shock on Miss Glory's long, sallow face.

'That's not nice,' she said. 'My dear, that isn't nice.'

'Well, didn't I tell you?' Cressida said weakly.

'But I think you're blaming the wrong person. That nice young Mr. Winter wouldn't do a thing like that.'

'He was the only one who knew I was looking for Lucy's death notice.'

'Aren't you underestimating Arabia?' Miss

Glory, was, as a sea captain's daughter, exercising her right to speak of Arabia as an equal.' She's a bad old woman, if you ask me. A really bad old woman.'

'I don't agree.' Cressida was instantly hotly loyal to the picturesque old woman who had been so kind to her.

'Of course she is. Hasn't she been leading you up the garden path about Lucy's purity and innocence? Goodness, no girl with all those boy friends would be likely to remain as pure as that.'

'She loved Lucy,' Cressida protested. 'It would be natural to protect her memory.'

'She does it because it amuses her. She would do anything for amusement, sell her own soul.' The dramatic words in Miss Glory's flat voice were almost comical. 'You mark my words, this is how she's decided to amuse herself with you. I've been her butt for long enough. I know.'

'Last night she was frightened,' Cressida whispered.

'Not her. She was acting. You listen to me, dear. I know her better than you. She'll feed you with cake and kisses, but she'll all the time be thinking out some other way to get a laugh out of you. But never mind,' Miss Glory patted Cressida's hand, 'she's harmless. She wouldn't actually carry out that notice. And I'm only telling you this because I don't think you should blame that nice Mr. Winter. Now I must go or someone,' suddenly she was coy, 'will be shouting for his morning tea. Don't you worry, dear. You stay here and ignore these little pranks like I do. They don't mean a thing.'

They certainly didn't seem to worry Miss

Glory, for a little later Cressida heard shrieks of laughter, and looked out to see Miss Glory, all feet and elbows, attempting to follow Mr. Moretti's smooth and skilful figure in a crazy rumba. The noise brought Mrs. Stanhope and Dawson to the head of the stairs. Dawson looked for a moment, then shrugged his thin shoulders contemptuously, and hurried off on his way to work. Mrs. Stanhope stood with a fixed smile, whether of amusement or pain Cressida couldn't decide. But in a moment she was shouldered aside by Arabia, who, in a crimson velvet dressing-gown trimmed lavishly with swansdown, stood at the head of the stairs and shouted encouragement.

She was neither the sad and apprehensive old woman of last night nor the practical joker with an unpleasant sense of the macabre. She was an energetic and enthusiastic figure on the point of joining in the crazy dance herself. Her foot tapped, her long, still graceful body swayed.

'Do you think this place is a night-club!' she called in her rich humorous voice. 'Gloriana Becker, do you call that dancing? Your feet are ten inches too long, and you put them down flat. On your toes, woman. Look, I'll show you.' She came down the stairs, her cheeks flushed, her fine eyes gleaming, and summarily took Mr. Moretti from Miss Glory. Mr. Moretti laughed, his mouth a dark cavern in the smooth colourlessness of his face. He guided Arabia across the marble floor, and she, her wide sleeves flowing back from her thin wrists, her grey head held high, moved with accomplished grace.

Then, laughing with the confidence of the

much-admired woman, she turned to the still breathless Miss Glory.

'I almost begin to see what you see in him. He dances like an angel. But you, my dear—must you really wear those boats on your feet, to begin with?'

'They're the feet I was born with,' Miss Glory retorted haughtily.

'Yes, but even the Almighty must sometimes wish He had a second chance over some of His creations.' Arabia threw back her head and gave her rich chuckle. 'Oh, this is fun. I haven't had so much fun since my second husband, who danced exquisitely, died. Cressida, my dear, I'm sure you dance beautifully.'

'I must be going to work,' Cressida said hastily. From a rumba to a requiem ... No one was saying the words aloud now, but Vincent Moretti's pale eyes were on her, and it was as if he were repeating them silently. Why?

'And I to practise,' he said in his smooth pleasant voice. 'Dear lady, that dance was delightful.'

'Oh, we'll have more,' Arabia said pleasurably. 'We're having a party for Cressida. We'll all dance.'

Cressida heard Jeremy Winter's low voice behind her.

'That was a very extraordinary thing to believe that I would do.'

Cressida moved sharply away. 'Then who did? Who did?' For it was impossible to believe that Arabia, with her warm abundant charm and gaiety, could have done so grotesque a thing.

'And there is no record of Lucy's death, if that

106

interests you,' Jeremy said in her ear, and then, as silently as he had come, went back down the basement stairs.

Cressida went back into her room to get her hat and coat. As she left the house the sombre melody of Massenet's Elegy played on the violin followed her. And on the steps outside Dawson was waiting.

It was foggy and the air was chilly. The brief gaiety of the dancing was forgotten, and now everything was grey. How could there be no record of Lucy's death? Had she been murdered and her murder forever concealed? The wail of the violin seeped through the heavy door, as if it were the theme song to this grey day.

'I waited for you, Miss Barclay,' Dawson said brightly.

'That was nice of you,' Cressida said with mechanical politeness. 'Didn't you like the dancing?'

'I think that Mr. Moretti is crazy,' Dawson said with sudden vindictiveness.

'Why? Because he wants to dance at nine o'clock in the morning?'

'Because he makes up to Miss Glory like that. He doesn't mean it and he's making a fool of her.'

'Dawson, how old are you?'

'Fifteen.' The boy was suddenly sullen again. 'But that doesn't mean I don't notice things.'

'Perhaps you notice too much. After all, Miss Glory is very happy, and if Mr. Moretti doesn't mean any harm—' How could he, to so coy and unattractive a woman?

'But he does! He's the sort of person who always means harm!'

107

'Oh, come,' said Cressida. 'I think you read too many sensational stories in the newspapers. What do you think he's planning to do to her? Seduce her and steal her money?'

'That's just the sort of thing he would do. And you mark my words, Miss Barclay, you won't be safe either!'

'Me!' Cressida gave a laugh of incredulity.

'You're pretty. He's probably got his eye on you already.'

'Oh, Dawson! You do let your imagination run away with you.' But already, inevitably, she was beginning to wonder whether Vincent Moretti were the mischief-maker. 'You think too much about morbid things, you know.'

'I'm interested in murders,' Dawson told her in his intense way. 'I like studying the way they're done. Now the girl who was strangled, you'd think that was a clumsy sort of way to commit murder, but it wasn't, really, because the police haven't got the murderer yet. He'd be a stranger, you see, and they've no way of connecting him with the girl.'

'Dawson! Do you talk to your poor little mother like this? No wonder she has nightmares.'

Dawson gave an abashed grin. 'It's just that I'm interested, Miss Barclay. And Ma doesn't really mind. She says I've got a legal mind.'

What would Dawson make of that charming little *billet-doux* she had received this morning? Cressida was almost tempted to tell him, but thought of the unnatural gleam that would come into his large myopic eyes, and refrained. No, she couldn't let Dawson gloat over her misfortunes. But it hadn't been Arabia who had sent the death notice. She couldn't convince herself that Arabia was guilty.

From a rumba to a requiem ... What was the meaning of that significant look in Mr. Moretti's eyes? Was he just ogling her, as he shamelessly ogled Miss Glory? Was Dawson right in warning her against him?

Or was Jeremy, who, after all, was the only one who knew of her secret activities, the scapegoat?

The day remained grey and cold, and even Mr. Mullins's habitual cheerfulness failed to make Cressida feel happy. She should be home with Tom, she should have listened to him and given up her ambitious ideas of independence. She could still go home to Tom and tell herself it was nonsense to imagine that she was chained because of a wistful lonely look in Arabia's eyes, and because the unfinished story of a dead girl challenged her.

'Is he making you unhappy already?' Mr. Mullins teased.

'Who?'

'Mr. Winter, of course.'

'Mr. Winter couldn't interest me less.'

Mr. Mullins gave his gentle knowing smile. Cressida's depression deepened, and with it her anger against Jeremy grew. Perhaps she had been unfair to him this morning, but even if he hadn't played that dastardly joke, why was he always dogging her footsteps? She was tired of it. She retired to the back of the shop to go through the accumulation of things in the large Victorian writing-desk which Mr. Mullins had said had been Arabia's

Really, Mr. Mullins was a muddler. It was true

that he made some brilliant sales, but he didn't know the half of his stock. Here, in these drawers, were porcelain figures, a Battersea enamel snuffbox, a lustre jug. There were books, too, and silver photograph frames, most of them empty, some showing faded pictures of long-dead people. It was pathetic the way people sold frames without bothering to take the pictures of their dead relatives out first. Who was this soldier in the uniform of the late nineteenth century? And this Victorian wedding group? Here was a much more recent wedding. The bride wore a comparatively modern wedding dress, and the groom didn't look quite so wooden as some of his predecessors. The photograph was in an elaborate silver frame and on the back was written—No, no!

Cressida dropped the picture as if it were red hot. It clattered on to the floor, and Mr. Mullins came pottering along among the dusty furniture, his pink face enquiring.

'Any damage, my dear? You didn't break anything?'

'No. I don't think so. Perhaps the glass—' Cressida was breathless. The photograph had fallen face downwards, and the scrawled words across the back were plainly visible.

'To darling Mummy, from Lucy and Larry. With all our love.'

It was Lucy's wedding photograph. Dead Lucy who had been buried in her ball dress, and clasping a posy of red roses, before her wedding day!

'It's Lucy,' Cressida heard herself whispering.

'So it is.' Mr. Mullins stooped to pick up the photograph. He looked at it consideringly. 'She was a pretty girl, but she hadn't a tenth of her mother's personality and distinction. You can see it there. Just a nice, attractive, ordinary girl. The young man looks a nice ordinary type, too.'

'But she didn't marry him!' Cressida cried. 'She didn't.'

Mr. Mullins looked at her enquiringly. His eyes were perplexed.

'It shows it there, my dear. Or isn't that Lucy at all?'

'Yes, it is. It's the same girl as in the photograph Arabia has. But she didn't marry Larry, Mr. Mullins. She wrote in her diary "Must order flowers" and it turned out that the flowers were for her funeral instead of her wedding.'

Because Lucy had died in an unnecessary and sordid way, keeping it secret from Larry that she had been going to have another man's child. That was what Arabia, dry-eyed and harrowed with pain and remorse, had admitted last night, and that was what Cressida had believed.

Yet here was evidence to prove that it had all been a lie.

Then why Arabia's grief, why the unused baby's glove, why the unfinished letter with its cry to an unknown lover, 'Darling, darling, darling...'?

For here was Lucy happily married.

Suddenly, aware of Mr. Mullins's interest, Cressida knew that she had been meant to find this photograph. He had not, from loyalty to his old friend Arabia, been going to tell her anything himself, but he had wanted her to have this evidence. It was to warn her against something. Against what? Perhaps Mr. Mullins himself didn't know. But there it was, the picture of the smiling bride and the tall, undistinguished but honest-looking young groom.

Well, this at least explained why Jeremy had found no record of Lucy's death. Because at the time of her death she hadn't been Lucy Bolton at all. She had been Lucy Meredith, Larry's wife.

Abruptly Cressida began to shiver. She said violently, 'Arabia shouldn't be so careless with her photographs. She can never have meant to leave this in the desk.'

'With Arabia one never knows,' Mr. Mullins said reflectively. 'If she perhaps didn't like the young man or approve of the marriage—'

'But she did! It was the other one she didn't approve of.'

'The other one?'

Cressida pulled herself up.

'Oh, Mr. Mullins, I'm sorry. I'm getting altogether too obsessed with Lucy. She seems to haunt me. What does it matter to me who she married, or whether she even married at all. She's dead, and it's all so long ago. Let's not show this to Arabia. It will only distress her. Let's forget all about it.'

'If you think it wise,' said Mr. Mullins.

'Of course it's wise. Why shouldn't it be? Why should I let a dead girl interfere in my life like this? I'll put her back in the dust, where she belongs.'

She hastily pushed the photograph behind a pile of old pictures, unsaleable, and likely to remain unmoved as long as Mr. Mullins had that

112

shop. It was almost as safe as a grave.

But Lucy had no grave...

★   ★   ★

That was the night footsteps followed Cressida home. The fog, lurking about all day, had deepened, and once out of the well-lighted areas it was impossible to see more than a yard ahead. As Cressida became aware of the persistent footsteps she found herself vainly regretting that she hadn't accepted Dawson's offer to see her home at nights. He might not be very prepossessing, nor, indeed, very courageous, but at least he would constitute an escort who would discourage this kind of thing.

Thanks to Dawson, however, she kept thinking of the girl strangled in the red shoes. That had happened not very far from here. Was this footstep, just beyond the reach of her vision in the fog, that of some madman who struck indiscriminately, or did it belong to someone who knew her and where she was going, and was purposely following her in this terrifying way?

Dragon House began to seem like a haven of peace and safety. She reached forward in her mind towards the comfortable flat that Arabia had prepared for her, the unknown girl who was to take dead Lucy's place. It didn't matter now what odd and humourless pranks were played on her in that house. They were harmless compared to this menace, this *pad, pad, pad* behind her in the fog.

It was in the moment after she had spun round to face her unknown follower, and he had stood there silent and invisible in the fog, that Cressida

113

panicked and ran. Her heart was bursting, her breath coming in great gasps, when at last she reached Dragon House, climbed the slippery marble steps and flung herself inside.

There was no one in the hall, but it was lighted and safe. A little ashamed now of her panic, she made her way to her own rooms. Reassuringly they were the same as she had left them that morning—no letters, no strange disturbing messages, no—Was that the front door opening and closing very softly?

Cressida, in a reflex action, switched off her light and made her way noiselessly to her own door which she had left ajar. In the same moment something sprang at her and she was caught in a tenacious grip round one ankle.

She couldn't control herself then. She screamed.

And the next moment the light flashed on and there stood Jeremy Winter laughing at her, while Mimosa relinquished his grip on her ankle and bounded away on a skittish game of his own.

'Sorry,' said Jeremy. 'Did he frighten you? He gets like this on foggy nights, I don't know why. Why, my dear child, you're trembling.'

'I thought—some horror—had followed me in out of the fog,' Cressida gasped. 'Actually someone did follow me home, and I thought just now I heard the front door open and shut...'

Her voice died away as she saw the moisture on Jeremy's hair and face. He must have just come in from outdoors himself. Her gaze travelled downwards hypnotically, and she saw on his feet heavy rubber-soled shoes.

'Someone followed you? That was unpleasant.'

114

'Yes,' said Cressida vaguely, looking at the slight damp marks his shoes had made on the marble floor.

'Well, don't imagine it was me,' said Jeremy. 'I've got a cold and haven't been out all day.' He paused to sneeze violently. 'Except just now when I went down to the corner to get milk for Mimosa.' He exhibited the bottle of milk with an air of innocence. 'Does that give me an alibi?'

'Don't joke about it!' Cressida said tensely. 'It wasn't funny, and I'm getting a little tired of unfunny jokes.'

'And I,' said Jeremy, 'am getting more than a little tired of being under suspicion. When anything unpleasant happens why do you instantly associate me with it? I can tell you, it hurts.'

He looked at her fiercely, his black eyebrows drawn now in a tight line so that his face was changed—it was that of an angry stranger.

'Well, it hurts, too, when people send me notices saying that I am dead. And it isn't exactly my idea of fun being followed home in a fog.'

'If you would ask for my help instead of accusing me—'

'I don't want your help,' Cressida cut in hotly. 'You only laugh at me, anyway. You think I imagine things. You really think I'm just a simple country girl who might provide you with a little harmless amusement because I'm naïve.'

'Naïve isn't quite the word I would use.' Jeremy's anger had vanished as quickly as it had come, and now his eyes had their irritating twinkle of mirth again. 'I could think of several more fitting ones.'

'Don't bother,' said Cressida frigidly. 'Don't

115

waste your valuable time thinking of me at all.'

Jeremy sneezed again and apologised.

'If I hadn't got this filthy cold I wouldn't, I'd kiss you instead. No wonder you were followed, you're much too attractive.'

Then he was gone, before Cressida could think of anything more to say. Mimosa bounded after him, a large, orange-coloured shadow, and Cressida was left, now no longer frightened, but suddenly oddly forlorn.

It wasn't going to be much fun living here if she kept quarrelling with Jeremy. She had wanted to tell him about her discovery of Lucy's wedding, but now she couldn't. Pride would not allow her to confide in him any more. She would have to struggle with Lucy's mysterious story by herself.

Now, more than ever, it demanded to be written. It must be because Arabia had not approved of Larry that she had refused to talk of Lucy's wedding, preferring Cressida to think she had died unmarried. Then had the coming baby been Larry's, too?

Cressida pulled open the drawer of her desk to take out her notes and add to them. Then she had one more shock on that oddest of all days. For her notes were torn into small pieces and left deliberately scattered in the drawer so that she could not fail to see their destruction.

CHAPTER TEN

It was then that Cressida felt she could stand no more. She was being persecuted in a mean and sly

116

way by someone who obviously was a little unbalanced. She had to admit it then, it did seem as if it must be Arabia who was doing these apparently senseless things. Already she had told a great many lies about Lucy, so it was clear that she was not to be relied on.

But Cressida had the greatest reluctance about believing these things of Arabia. The old lady was so gallant, so amusing, so decorative. It was terrible to think that all the time she was pretending to be a friend she was doing these nasty malicious things. All the same, it stood to reason. No one who was entirely sane would go about wearing a valuable tiara, for instance. Eccentricity was a charitable name for whatever afflicted Arabia, but it wasn't nice at all to reflect that her malady might be more serious than that.

Cressida made an omelet for her evening meal and ate it without being aware of what she was doing. By that time she had come to her decision, and reluctantly she sat down to write to Tom.

'Dear Tom,
Thank you for your letter this morning which I was very pleased to get. I'm sorry I didn't write yesterday, but all sorts of things were happening. Some of them were odd mysterious things, which I am sure you wouldn't like, and when I tell you what has happened today I think you will agree that I am right in not staying here after all...'

Were Cressida hesitated, suddenly at a loss as to how to put into words her sensation of fear and apprehension, both about her notes on Lucy being torn up and those footsteps padding behind her in the fog. Then all at once she had an illuminating thought, and suddenly she was happy and light-hearted.

For it couldn't be Arabia who was playing these tricks on her. How could an old woman follow her briskly down the street? At the end she had been running, and yet her pursuer had lightly kept pace with her. How could Arabia, in her seventy-fifth year, run like that, even had she been so crazy as to try?

Anything that had happened in the house would have been within Arabia's capabilities, but not that pursuing trick. And why should she imagine that different people had done the different things? No, it must be all the work of one person, someone who hated her or who was jealous of her, or who just had a nasty malicious mind.

If it was not Arabia she was not going to leave Dragon House. For, if someone here were behaving in that unbalanced way, Arabia more than ever had need of her.

But who could it be?

Cressida tore up the letter to Tom, and began again.

'Dear Tom,

I am having such an exciting and absorbing time here that I am sorry I didn't even get round to writing to you yesterday. Please forgive me for this, but if you knew—'

Here she had to stop, for there was an urgent knocking at her door. When she opened it (with some trepidation, for she had begun to wonder what next to expect) Dawson stood there, looking pale and agitated.

'Oh, Miss Barclay, could you come up and see Ma, she's sick,' he said all in one breath.

'Why, of course I will, Dawson. But I don't know very much about illnesses. What do you think is the matter?'

'She's sick, and she's got bad pains.' The boy, for all his professed experience with minor illnesses and remedies, was obviously frightened.

'It sounds like an appendicitis,' Cressida said. 'I think Miss Glory might be of more use than me.'

'No, Ma said you,' Dawson urged, beginning to lead the way up the stairs.

Cressida followed him with some reluctance. It was true that she had had little experience with illness, and Mrs. Stanhope sounded as if she required professional attention. She went into the room, dimly lit by the bedside light only, and saw the sick woman lying small and very white on the divan bed.

'I'm feeling a little better now,' Mrs. Stanhope whispered, as Cressida bent over her.

'Can I do anything for you? Shall I send for a doctor?' Cressida asked anxiously.

Mrs. Stanhope shook her head. Her hair lay in damp wisps on the pillow, her little triangular face had a tired defenceless look.

'No, I'm better now,' she said in her hoarse voice. 'I don't need a doctor.'

'But are you sure—'

'No, no, I don't want a doctor,' Mrs. Stanhope whispered emphatically. Then she raised herself on her elbow and beckoned to Dawson, who was

119

standing in the shadows, to give her her writing pad and pencil. He did so, and in a large shaky hand she wrote, 'I had tea with Mrs. Bolton.'

'Oh, yes,' said Cressida politely. Mrs. Stanhope was watching her with a curious expectancy, so she added, 'Were you all right then? Did this attack come on afterwards?'

Mrs. Stanhope nodded. Her eyes held a look of fear—or was it triumph? Behind her, Cressida heard Dawson saying, 'Ma thinks it was something she ate at Mrs. Bolton's that upset her.'

'Oh, that was bad luck,' said Cressida.

Mrs. Stanhope wrote feverishly on her everlasting pad, 'Dawson gave me an antidote. He knows about these things.' She displayed the scrawled writing to Cressida, then added, almost with a flourish, 'It was lucky he come home in time.'

Cressida lifted shocked eyes. She looked at the little woman, pitiably thin and white, the crushed ruffles of her nightdress coming modestly round her tiny bony neck, then turned to the gangling boy behind her, who said off-handedly,

'I keep remedies for simple troubles—coughs and colds and headaches and rheumatism, and upset stomachs. Of course if it's poisoning it can be more complicated, but I think Ma will be all right now.'

Sudden swift anger took hold of Cressida. She found herself comparing Arabia, warm-hearted, colourful, bringing her cluttered rooms alive with her tremendous vitality, with this pitiable pair—Mrs. Stanhope weak and complaining, Dawson under-developed, over-grown and unbearably smug. That they could even hint at such a thing was intolerable. Moreover, it was fantastic and quite unbelievable.

'I don't know why you sent for me,' she said stiffly. 'You say you're better now and there's nothing I can do, so I'll go and let you get some sleep.'

'No, wait!' Mrs. Stanhope had her writing pad again, and was scribbling rapidly. 'I asked you to come up here because I thought you ought to know this.' She paused to look up at Cressida with significant eyes. Then she wrote, 'You will be seeing more of Mrs. Bolton than any of us. I wanted to warn you.'

Cressida tore the sheet of paper off the pad and screwed it up angrily.

'I don't believe it,' she said flatly.

'Ma said it was the liqueur cake,' Dawson said in his detached way. 'That would have a strong flavour, and could conceal another taste.'

'Oh, I think you're intolerable!' Cressida cried. 'I'm sorry you've been ill, Mrs. Stanhope, but I just refuse to believe anything so monstrous. I expect it was simply that the liqueur cake was too rich for you.'

Then they both seemed to be looking at her with pity, almost as if it were she lying ill on the bed, stricken down by Arabia's wicked machinations. The thing was a nightmare. She would not tolerate the thought of it.

Cressida backed to the door. Dawson's voice followed her.

'I think you ought to listen to us more, Miss Barclay. You did get locked in that room the other night, remember? Common sense points out that only one person could have done a thing like that, and that would be a person who wasn't quite *compos mentis*, if you know what I mean.'

'I know very well, and I still think you're making the most unjustified slanders. In fact, to prove you're wrong, I'm going up now to have a piece of that cake myself.'

'Miss Barclay, Miss Barclay!' came the hoarse whisper from the bed. 'We're only warning you for your own good. You ought to listen.'

'Yes, you should,' said Dawson. 'The pattern of Mrs. Bolton's behaviour all points to—'

Cressida couldn't listen any more. She knew that Dawson was going to use some long medical term, and that his mother was whispering proudly that Dawson had a legal mind. She shut the door on the odd and more than a little pathetic pair, and went slowly along the passage to Arabia's suite of rooms.

It was true that Arabia did do strange things, of course. Who else could it have been who had locked her in Lucy's room, or who indeed who had torn up her notes? Arabia's guilt and despair over Lucy's death could well have left her a little unbalanced. While genuinely growing fond of Cressida, she could have resented the very fact that Cressida was alive while Lucy was dead. That could have prompted her to send that death notice, and do other equally extraordinary things.

But why should her malice extend to an innocent and harmless person like Mrs. Stanhope? Miss Glory had said that Arabia would do anything at all to amuse herself, even the most bizarre and thoughtless things. But surely mildly poisoning a guest could not be termed

122

amusement!

No, that was a myth that existed only in Mrs. Stanhope's mind. She had been upset by the rich cake, and Dawson, anxious to experiment with his small amount of medical knowledge, had encouraged her to believe that she was very ill. That was all it was.

Reassured by this common-sense explanation, Cressida knocked briefly on Arabia's door, and immediately the deep rich voice of the old woman bade her enter.

The room was full of rosy light. All the lamps were alight—the three standard ones with their wide, scarlet shades, and the two exquisite Chinese porcelain ones that stood on the mantelpiece. In this pool of warmth Arabia sat, the rainbow cushions scattered about her, the jewels in her tiara shining splendidly. She was like an oriental queen reposing on her couch among all this haphazard splendour. She was very different from the remorse-ridden old woman in bed last night, confessing her tragic secret. Tonight, Cressida sensed, was one of the occasions when she had put the past out of her mind, and was being her other self, Arabia the great, the irresistible, the glamorous, the unshockable.

She was, perhaps, a little mad, but it was a glorious madness. In that moment Cressida knew that she adored her, and could not refuse her anything, even the years of her life that would take her to the time of Arabia's death.

Perhaps she was a little mad herself, but she knew that, like Arabia, she worshipped the warm and colourful things in life, the diverting, the exquisite and impractical.

'My dear, my dear!' Arabia cried in delighted welcome. 'I thought you might call on a lonely old woman, so I dressed for you.' She spread the stiff brocade skirts of her dinner gown. 'This is the dress my third husband used to like me to wear to the formal dinners we had given for us on our return from an expedition. We were celebrities then. We had parties at the Ritz and the Savoy, and absolutely everyone used to be there, even royalty. I got this material in a bazaar in Baghdad. It's quite indestructible. The sheik used to say—well, never mind that now. Come and tell me about your day. Is Mr. Mullins being kind to you? If he isn't I shall take that clock back. Oh, my dear, weren't we crazy this morning, dancing like that. But I must say for Moretti he has a light foot, even if I do feel his eyebrows will crawl on to me at any moment.'

Arabia gave her rich peal of laughter, and Ahmed, on his perch, croaked sleepily. The room was full of a heavy perfume that was a mixture of gardenia and spice. It made Cressida feel slightly but pleasurably intoxicated.

'It made me feel forty-one—well, perhaps forty-five. Though I rode on a mule through an Afghanistan pass at sixty-nine, and was none the worse for it. The sheik, when I told him, said he would bet me twenty camels that it wasn't true, and how was I to prove it? None of those Mongolians could speak a word of English. That was when I saw all those vultures—My dear, don't let me run on like this. Are you hungry? Will you take a little supper with me? Of course you will. I'll make some hot chocolate. No need

124

to get Miss Glory up. Those large feet of hers. She treads on so much *ground*!'

'I'd love a piece of your liqueur cake,' Cressida said.

Arabia eyed her benignly.

'And where have you heard about my liqueur cake? Did someone tell you it was my speciality? The sheik said it was divine, and that he would happily make me his tenth wife if I made it for him every day. Small chance he had. Those nine other wives would have gobbled it up before he had a chance to look at it. And me, too, most likely. Certainly you shall have a piece of my liqueur cake, my dear. Just one moment while I put the kettle on.'

Arabia trailed into the kitchen, the long skirts of her gown rustling. Dishes began to clatter, and snatches of song floated out. Arabia was in a particularly gay mood tonight—was it because she had enjoyed playing a dangerous prank on Mrs. Stanhope?

Pale hands I loved beside the Shalimar ... came the deep musical voice. The fire crackled lightly, Ahmed ruffled his feathers and slept again, the lights glowed cosily in the warm, friendly room.

'I had that wretched little Stanhope woman to tea this afternoon,' Arabia said presently. 'I thought I ought to be kind to her, but goodness gracious, that scribbling block of hers! It was like entertaining the Elgin Marbles.'

Cressida began to laugh with pleasure. Arabia was wonderful, she was adorable.

'I thought I might have been able to wrest some amusement from her,' Arabia went on. 'Usually there is some way, with even the most

125

unpromising material. But no! Not when one spends one's time reading the most banal remarks. The doctor has forbidden her to speak for three months, apparently, so that she can avoid having a throat operation. I don't really think the world is missing much by the little Stanhope's loss of voice. My dear, here is the cake!'

Arabia trailed into the room again, and handed Cressida a plate on which was a large slice of rich and creamy cake.

'Eat it all, darling. It's saturated in brandy. It will do you good. It made the little Stanhope very garrulous with her pencil and pad. Oh dear, I suppose I should be more charitable. But I do insist that people be amusing.'

'Mrs. Stanhope isn't very well tonight,' Cressida remarked off-handedly. She began to eat the cake, because how could there be anything wrong with it when Arabia had so unquestioningly produced it. That proved what nonsense the Stanhopes talked.

'I'm not surprised at that. She was extremely greedy this afternoon. I think she probably starves herself, poor scrap. Her husband deserted her, you know (not that I blame him), and she's had to fend for herself and bring up that drainpipe of a boy. That's why I let her have the rooms. I get absurdly soft-hearted at times, and then I regret it. Eat up your cake, my love. There's plenty more. If you like it we'll have one for your party.'

'It's delicious,' said Cressida with truth.

Arabia gave her radiant smile.

'You are a sweet child. Really, my dear, I love you so much. Is that foolish of me?'

It was a wicked scandal that Mrs. Stanhope should accuse Arabia of trying to poison her. She might indeed play pranks to provide herself with the diversions she found so necessary, but she would not do anything dangerous.

Cressida, finishing her cake with complete trust, said simply, 'I love you, too.'

'Oh, my dear!' The hooded eyelids fell to cover the quick gleam of tears. Then the heavily ringed fingers, like dry old twigs improbably bursting into bloom, patted Cressida's hand. The old lady was obviously overcome with sudden emotion.

Presently she said, 'Forgive me, I wanted to cry a little. It's so long since I have been happy like this.'

'You've grieved for Lucy too long,' Cressida said.

'I know I have. One can waste too much of one's life on grief and remorse. Useless emotions, both of them. I like to be gay and happy, to laugh and sing. And from this moment I am going to be happy. Away with the past. Away with remorse. Life shall begin again.' Arabia sprang up energetically and ruffled Ahmed's feathers. He squawked bad-temperedly, and she gave her deep peal of laughter. 'Eh, you don't like that, you old vulture. You don't like your mistress growing young and skittish again. But she's happy, she's happy.'

'Arabia,' Cressida began tentatively. 'It was true what you told me about Lucy, wasn't it?'

Arabia was suddenly still. She stood, a tall, dramatic figure with Ahmed on her shoulder, just outside the rosy circle of light.

'And why should I tell you lies?' she asked

127

haughtily.

'I mean about the way Lucy died,' Cressida persisted, thinking of the photograph which she was now sure Mr. Mullins had meant her to find. For why should Lucy die in that miserable, tragic way if she had indeed been happily married?

Arabia began to speak rapidly. 'I admit that in the past I have misled people about Lucy's death. Perhaps she was not entirely the pure young girl I had suggested. Perhaps things had happened. What was it more than life, after all? But I had loved her so much and I was so shocked and grieved, I was nearly mad for a while. So I built up this fairy-tale nonsense—not nonsense, entirely, for it was that way at the beginning. Lucy was sweet and loving and innocent until—no, no, I won't talk about it. From now on it's a closed book.'

'But, Arabia dear, I want to know—'

Arabia swiftly crossed over to Cressida and put her fingers over her lips.

'Not another word, my dear. I have been very wrong to let Lucy haunt your life like this. At first you reminded me of her so much my silly old mind got confused; I mixed present and past. But no more of that. You are yourself and you mustn't live a dead girl's life. I've come to a momentous decision. I've begun to dismantle that room upstairs. I've been morbid for too long, and I almost made you morbid, too. Mr. Mullins might like some of the things. The bedside lamp—I gave it to Lucy on her seventeenth birthday. Have you noticed it? It's an early Meissen figure. Lucy was enchanted with it. I remember—But, no, no more of that.'

'Please go on. I like to hear it.' Anything, even the expensive bedside lamp and Lucy's youthful pleasure, might lead to the reason for her tragic end.

Arabia shook her head decisively. Her craggy old face had lost its softness and was suddenly stubborn and forbidding.

'Not another word. Lucy is buried at last, and at peace.'

'But won't you ever tell me any more about her? Not about Larry, even? She was in love with Larry, wasn't she?'

'I thought so, but a young girl's mind can be devious, devious and changeable.'

'But the baby—'

'I've told you! Now hold your tongue about it!'

It was the first time Arabia had spoken harshly to Cressida. There was no doubting that she meant what she said. The enthralling subject of Lucy, which she had lived on for nearly twenty years, was now closed. It was hard to believe, but it was true. Cressida was to hear nothing more about that enigmatic young girl who had lived light-heartedly and recklessly, and then had prepared for the birth of a baby that was destined not to be born. Arabia, who had been so garrulous, was suddenly going to be exasperatingly silent. Why? Did she truly want to put Lucy out of her mind forever, or was she afraid that Cressida was beginning to discover too much?

Arabia, with her rapid and fascinating changes of mood, was suddenly laughing, her sparkling eyes willing Cressida to do the same.

'Darling child, don't look so angry and
129

frustrated. Lucy is nothing to you. You are yourself. You have nothing but a name in common.'

'But I wanted to write a story about her,' Cressida said. 'It was going to be such an absorbing story—the ball dresses, the red roses, the half-finished diary, the unanswered invitations, the men she loved—'

'Why do you say men?' Then Arabia, obviously regretting her involuntary question which would have led to further revelations, went on, 'Now you have found out how Lucy died her story is no longer innocent and beautiful, so we will speak of it no more. It distresses me too much. We will talk of other things. Won't you have another piece of cake?'

Cressida looked at her empty plate. Without thinking, she had eaten the whole of the cake Arabia had given her, and she felt perfectly well. As of course she would. It was ridiculous to think otherwise.

Was it when Arabia had begun dismantling that pretty petrified room upstairs that she had thought to go down to Cressida's flat and destroy the notes about Lucy? If that were the simple explanation to that piece of vandalism, then it must merely have been a street prowler who had followed her home. And with Lucy metaphorically buried at last the other senseless and macabre pranks would also cease. So she could really write truthfully to Tom that Dragon House was a pleasant and friendly place in which to live.

'I intend to remake my will,' Arabia said, startling Cressida out of her reflections.

She looked up with sudden apprehension.

Arabia gave her warm embracing smile and said compellingly.

'So boring, leaving one's money to strangers. You will allow me to give you a little, won't you?'

'Oh, no! Please!'

'But why not? It would give me so much pleasure.'

'No. Tom wouldn't allow it.'

Arabia drew herself up. 'Tom, I fear, is a very domineering young man. Are you really in love with him?'

'I—why, yes—'

'Frankly, I don't see how you can be. An adding machine, an account book, the "if one and one make two, then two and two must make four" variety. But two and two don't always make four. Sometimes they make five. Isn't it *interesting*?'

Cressida, under the fascinating old creature's spell, could say nothing.

'I don't think your Tom has ever discovered that life can be full of the most wonderful surprises. And if you produced the surprises, I fear he would argue that they didn't exist, that they were an hallucination. Am I right?'

'Well—'

'You dither, child. So I must be right. A fig for Tom and his opinions, then. Is there any other reason that I can't leave you a little of my money?'

'There would be—unpleasantness,' Cressida said reluctantly.

'Explain!'

'Among your relatives.' Now she was quoting both Tom and Jeremy. This, probably, was the only fact on which those two would ever agree.

'But I have none!' Arabia exclaimed triumphantly. 'Not a single mortal soul in the world. Not a twice-removed cousin or a step-sister or the illegitimate child of a great nephew. So where, may I ask, will the unpleasantness come from? Come, my dear, I have made up my mind about this. So make me happy by being delighted about it. I do so much like to give pleasure.'

'Me, too,' said Cressida, almost in a whisper. That, indeed, was her weakness. She could not bear to cause pain or disappointment. So how could she refuse to accept what Arabia wanted to give her? She would give all the money away, she privately decided, just as she had told Jeremy she would. And, anyway, this thing may never happen. Arabia looked as if she might live for ten or fifteen years yet; and in that time, in an uncertain world, her finances could completely alter. She might not, by then, be a wealthy woman at all.

'Then it's settled,' Arabia cried. 'I'll telephone my solicitor tomorrow. Oh, this has been a lovely, lovely evening. Now away to bed with you.'

CHAPTER ELEVEN

It was true that what Arabia planned to do did make her very happy. All her life she had done impulsive generous things, and they had always given her happiness. For a long time the knowledge that she had no one who really cared about her for herself had been like a cold stone in

132

her heart. Oh, plenty of people had been charming to her, with the thought in the back of their minds that the foolish old woman would have to die one day, and then perhaps they could acquire some of her money and promptly forget her.

But this girl was different. She breathed sincerity. When she had told Arabia that she loved her, she had meant it. Arabia had known too many people in her long life not to be able to recognise truth when she encountered it. Cressida was a dear sweet child, and fate had brought them together. The spring, no matter how brief it might be, had come back for these golden days. And a ghost had been exorcised.

Now she could sleep soundly, as she had not done for so long. The evil had gone out of the house.

Arabia went about turning out lights and humming spiritedly.

'You old vulture,' she said affectionately to Ahmed, and carried him in to stand on her bedpost.

Ahmed, who was likely to live to be a hundred and fifty, she would bequeath to Cressida too. He would take with him a little of her rich voluptuous past. He could not talk about it, but it would not matter if he could to Cressida, who would understand—except perhaps for that one thing. But that ghost was exorcised. There would be no more hissed voice in the quiet of the night. Now there was peace and springtime. It would last until the day of her death.

Tomorrow she must get in touch with her solicitor. And it would be a good idea to get Miss

133

Glory started on the preparations for the party. They would make another liqueur cake, since Cressida, bless her, had liked it so much. It served Mrs. Stanhope right if she had been ill that afternoon. She had been so greedy, eating up all she could get, and those eyes of hers, magnified behind the strong glasses, had roved round the room taking in everything. One had had the impression that her thin little hands had longed to seize things.

Ah well, poor scrap, she hadn't had much of a life. One must be kind. One could afford to be kind now that one was so happy. It would not be so difficult putting up with a bore.

Now Moretti, suddenly, had ceased to be a bore. He had definite possibilities. Those avid, light-coloured eyes, and his magical feet. Yes, there was amusement to be had there. The party on Saturday must start either very early or very late to enable Moretti to be there. Very late, perhaps. They could eat and drink and dance until daylight. The last time she had done that had been in Algiers—how long ago?—more than fifteen years. But she still remembered the moon setting and the roof-tops and minarets growing ghostly, and then pink-flushed as the light deepened. That was when she and that handsome French-Moroccan had driven to the outskirts of the city and hired camels and ridden before breakfast. Crazy days! The English had turned up their noses at camels. Nothing but the best horse-flesh for them. Ah, the heat, the smell, the sense of timelessness those old cities gave one...

But she had had to come back to this house finally. It was then she had thought to placate

Lucy by reopening that charming room upstairs and pretending that it was only awaiting an occupant. For fifteen years she had put fresh flowers on the dressing-table, and dusted and cleaned with her own hands. Sometimes she had spent hours in there imagining she could hear Lucy's laughter and her light happy voice, imagining the little slippers had Lucy's feet in them, or the bedclothes were thrown back to admit Lucy's slender body.

Now that kind of daydreaming was finished, for she had reality, not a ghost. Mr. Mullins would be asked to take away the lamp made from an old Meissen vase, the gilt-framed triple mirror, the period dressing-table and stool, the bed with its elaborately carved ends. The clothing she would have destroyed, and then the room, empty and anonymous, shut up. In this way Lucy's ghost would be gone forever. She had made a mistake in allowing it to remain for Cressida to become acquainted with it. But how was she to have known that Cressida would be so lovable and sincere?

No damage had been done. If Lucy were not talked about any more Cressida would quickly forget the story that haunted her. Her eager young mind would seize on something else. She would fall in love, not with that dull country cabbage, Tom, but with someone handsome and vital and amusing. There would be another wedding in Dragon House.

Another wedding ... Arabia's happy dreaming ceased. Lucy's ghost was not quite laid. There was just that tiny lingering thing, that doubt. The

135

knitted baby's sock. How had it got into Lucy's room? And why?

CHAPTER TWELVE

If Arabia were confident she would sleep soundly that night, Cressida found that she could not sleep at all.

Too much had happened. Her mind could no longer sanely examine and sift evidence. Evidence? Why had she used that word? What did she imagine had happened once in this old house? And if anything strange and perhaps terrible had happened, was she never to discover what it had been?

When Arabia said that in future there would be silence about Lucy, Cressida knew that she meant it. She suspected that even torture would not drag from the old woman any information which she did not wish to divulge. This was maddeningly exasperating, but it looked as if the story of Lucy were over. Unless she could find out anything more for herself.

She wondered for the twentieth time why she had this compelling urge to discover Lucy's story. It was as if Lucy's ghost stood over her, bidding her.

And tomorrow the room upstairs, the pretty girlish shrine kept for so long, was to be shut up. Gone would be the perfume of roses, the unfinished story, the sense of time stopped, of a sleeping beauty who was not there.

Cressida was aware of a curious sense of loss. She twisted uneasily in bed. The night was still. It was so late that only an occasional passing car disturbed the quiet. In the distance Cressida heard a clock striking. It was the clock from the spire of St. Mark's Church, she knew, and suddenly, as the slow chimes struck the hour of three o'clock, she had an idea. If Lucy had been married the marriage would almost certainly have taken place in St. Mark's, which was not only the nearest church, but a fashionable one for weddings. Tomorrow she would go and ask to see the marriage register. If nothing more, it would give her evidence of the wedding, but what she hoped for most was that it would give her Larry's address. Then she could go and see Larry.

The idea was brilliant! Lucy's widowed husband could answer all her questions. Why hadn't she thought before of finding him? But of course, silly, she told herself, you didn't know until yesterday that Lucy had married him.

She must not tell Arabia what she planned. Arabia would be deeply hurt, and would not understand the writer's urge that drove her. She must do this secretly. No one at all should know.

Having come to that decision, Cressida's mind was suddenly free and empty, and almost at once she went to sleep.

It seemed that there would always be noise to awake her in Dragon House. This morning it was a loud squawking from Ahmed, and then Arabia's urgent 'Shoo shoo! Vulture, vulture!' Cressida put on a dressing-gown and opened her door in time to see Mimosa streaking past and down the basement stairs, while Arabia wrathfully came down the stairs—Ahmed, ruffled and still muttering, on her shoulder.

'That cat!' Arabia declared. 'Stalking Ahmed is his favourite sport. You should see my drawing-room. Chaos! And my poor pretty here, frightened out of his wits. Come, sweetie, it's all right now. That devil had gone. Kiss Mamma.'

'Doesn't Jeremy stop him?' Cressida enquired.

'Not him. He thinks it's amusing. Gives him ideas, he says. Pah!'

But Jeremy had not witnessed the chase this morning. He did not appear, and Arabia, since she had no one with whom to quarrel, rapidly recovered her temper.

'By the way, Cressida darling, I mean to bequeath Ahmed to you, also. You will be kind to him, won't you? He responds so to affection. If he likes you he'll nibble your ear constantly. Ah, Dawson, good morning.' Dawson was coming down sleepily for the milk. 'Is your mother quite recovered?'

'Ma? Yes, she's all right.'

'I heard she was a little off-colour last night. Naughty soul, she'll have to behave better than that on Saturday night.'

Arabia departed, cooing to Ahmed, and Cressida said to Dawson, 'Is that true? Your mother really is better?'

'Practically, yes.'

'Then it was silly to imagine about the poison, wasn't it?'

Cressida's voice was quite friendly, but to her surprise Dawson shot her a sulky, angry look.

'I'm not that dumb, Miss Barclay. If I hadn't had the right remedy on hand I wouldn't like to say what would have happened.'

'Oh, Dawson, I'm sure you're very clever with

your remedies, but I think you like to dramatise a little, don't you? After all, I ate that cake last night and there was absolutely nothing wrong with it.'

'All right, don't believe me,' Dawson flared suddenly. 'But you'll be sorry one day.' He turned to go, but shot over his shoulder what to him was probably an excruciatingly funny remark, 'You mightn't even live long enough to have Ahmed nibbling at your ear.'

Was it chance that caused Vincent Moretti to appear at that moment? Cressida was beginning to think that everyone in Dragon House had a habit of eavesdropping.

'Extraordinary lad,' he commented to Cressida, as Dawson went back upstairs with the milk. 'What flight of fancy is he engaged on now?'

Impulsively Cressida said, 'Mr. Moretti, do you think Mrs. Bolton is a little eccentric? Well, more than a little?'

The thick fair eyebrows went up. Mr. Moretti's pale eyes were full of their secret knowledge.

'She did rumba rather nicely for a seventy-five-year-old, didn't she?'

'That doesn't prove anything. She would still ride a camel, too, if she had the opportunity.'

'That's what I mean.'

'Well, if that's the extent of her eccentricity, I think it's rather charming,' Cressida said loyally.

'Oh, indeed. We all have our little foibles. Mine is for dirges.' Mr. Moretti gave his wide smile. As at that moment Miss Glory approached with a tea tray he added quickly. 'But no dirge at this moment,' and began to sing passionately, '*My love is like a red, red rose...*'

From a rumba to a requiem ... A red, red rose...

139

No, no, she must get out of this habit of attaching significance to the smallest and most casual remark. The red, red rose was, improbably enough, Miss Glory, and Miss Glory was indeed blushing like a rose.

It was very naughty of Mr. Moretti to behave in this way, because Cressida was quite certain he didn't care in the least for Miss Glory. He was merely amusing himself, as Arabia amused herself, less harmfully, with people. But what was Miss Glory going to do when she discovered his insincerity?

The fog had not quite cleared, and its cool grey wraiths were drifting in the window. It was going to be one of those dreary, half-dark days that weighed on one's spirits as heavily as trouble. She would go down to St. Mark's Church in her lunch hour and look at the marriage register.

Miss Glory was forgotten. Lucy had stepped into Cressida's mind again.

*　　　*　　　*

When, four hours later, Cressida read the entry in the register, written plainly in thick black writing, it was as if Lucy had come to life. For there it was, indisputably, the record of the marriage of Cressida Lucy Bolton to Laurence Meredith of Sloane Street, Chelsea. Lucy had been twenty-one, Laurence twenty-five. The marriage had taken place nineteen years ago.

Cressida looked at the entry for a long time. Then, absently, she gave half-a-crown to the elderly verger and left the church. If she hurried there would be time to slip over to Chelsea. She would call at the house in Sloane Street and ask to see Larry. She had no idea what she was going to say to him, but that would come when she had actually set eyes on someone who previously had seemed a myth. Lucy's legitimate husband, Larry Meredith.

The fog had thickened and the air was dank and smelt of soot. Cressida longed suddenly for warm, lighted restaurants and cheerful voices. That place where she and Jeremy had lunched the other day—was it only two days ago? She had no taste for what she was doing, yet she was driven to it. What could Larry tell her about his long-dead wife?

The house was one of a terrace of tall, dignified, brick houses. After she had climbed the steps and pressed the well-polished bell, Cressida had a sudden moment of panic. Was this a very audacious and extraordinary thing to be doing?

She had not time to grow nervous, for the door opened and an elderly woman, obviously a housekeeper, looked at her enquiringly.

'Oh, I want to see Mr. Meredith, if I may. That is, if he still lives here.'

'I'm afraid the Merediths haven't lived here for a long time,' the woman answered rather coldly.

'Oh, haven't they? No, I suppose it's likely they haven't. After nineteen years—' Cressida was talking incomprehensibly. How silly she was to walk up to that door and imagine that Larry or his mother would open it, as they would have done nineteen years ago. Time went by, and people grew older and shifted their residences. How Jeremy would have scorned the ineptness of her plan that, half an hour ago, had seemed so brilliant.

She was aware of the woman's bewilderment and pulled herself together.

'I'm so sorry to trouble you, but I wonder if you know at all where they moved to. I particularly wanted to see Larry. I—' Nineteen years—hard as it was to imagine, Larry was not a boy any longer, he was in his middle forties. 'My mother used to know him very well, and while I'm in London she asked me to look him up,' Cressida quickly improvised.

The woman was definitely suspicious now. She said stiffly:

'You'll hardly be able to do that, miss, since he's been dead this fifteen years or more.'

'Dead!' Cressida whispered.

'That was when the Merediths moved, so I've heard, but I don't know the ins and outs of it.'

'Wasn't he—young to die?' Cressida got out. Was there a blight on everybody? Had they all died in their youth, the people of that long-ago spring?

A voice sounded behind the woman in the doorway.

'Is that someone wanting to see Larry Meredith's grave? Tell her it's in the cemetery down the Fulham Road. Ask the sexton. He'll show her.'

The speaker was an old cleaning woman, down on her knees polishing the floor. Before Cressida could catch more than a glimpse of her wrinkled, grinning face, the stout woman in the doorway gave her a brief nod of dismissal and closed the door.

And the fog had got right inside her, chilling

142

her so that she was shivering. There was only one thing that she was sure of in that moment. Larry, unlike Lucy, had a grave. She had to see it.

The taxi-driver seemed to think it a little odd that a young woman should choose to visit a cemetery in the dreary fog. Cressida, aware of him looking at her empty hands, knew that he was reflecting that she hadn't even any flowers. Not even a red rose, though he knew nothing about the significance of red roses.

She should not be spending the salary which Mr. Mullins had kindly advanced her on taxicabs, but this was important. Why it was important she could not have explained. It was just simply that as she had had to find out about Larry, now she had to see that his grave really existed.

Even with the help of the sexton it was difficult to find the grave, but finally they came upon it, and the sexton ambled off leaving her to look at the stone which bore the simple inscription, 'Laurence Meredith, dearly loved son of Clara and John Meredith. Aged twenty-nine years.'

That was all. Not dearly loved husband of Lucy Meredith. No mention of Lucy at all. In his death Larry was claimed only by his parents. He did not even lie beside his wife. His wife had no grave.

A low wind stirred dead leaves on the ground. A rook flapped its ebony way out of the fog. No voice spoke. No one told her where Lucy was, nor why Larry lay here so forlornly alone. Only the fog hung over the gravestones that were the same cold grey colour.

Abruptly the tears began to run down Cressida's cheeks. She longed to go home to Arabia's warm glowing room, to have Arabia's rich humorous voice in her ears, and the spell of Arabia's personality about her. Quickly, she had to forget this dreary churchyard with its fog-coloured gravestone, and its sad inscription.

From a rumba to a requiem ... But that had been Lucy. Lucy, not Larry...

*　　*　　*

Mr. Mullins raised his eyebrows at the lateness of her return from lunch. Fortunately there were several people in the shop, and Cressida was able to compose herself before an opportunity came to talk with Mr. Mullins.

Then she said, 'I'm sorry I was late, but there were several things I had to do, and they took so long.'

'Don't let your work interfere, of course,' Mr. Mullins said, with gentle sarcasm. Then he realised Cressida's distress, and said quickly, 'Is there something wrong, Miss Barclay? You have been crying! Ah, it's that Jeremy. He's been upsetting you.'

Jeremy—she hadn't seen him since yesterday morning. It seemed suddenly like years.

'Mr. Mullins,' she said urgently, 'did you know Larry was dead, too?'

'Larry?'

'The man Lucy Bolton married. You know, the photograph that we found yesterday.'

'Oh, that one. Well, goodness me, he well maybe by now.'

'But why? He would only be in his forties. He would be young still.'

'My dear, there has been a major war in the

interval.'

'But it wasn't in the war. It was the year before the war started.'

Cressida looked at Mr. Mullins's round, bland face.

'Did you know he was dead?' she demanded accusingly.

'My dear Miss Barclay, I know nothing about Arabia's family that she doesn't tell me, and this she has never told me.'

'But why? Why doesn't she talk about it?'

'That surely is her own business. I never ask questions about things that don't concern me.'

Mr. Mullins's voice was final. He turned to re-arrange the window, which had been disturbed by the sale of a Spode tea-service. Cressida followed him determinedly.

'But, Mr. Mullins, you meant me to find that photograph yesterday. Why did you do that if I'm not to be told anything more?'

'You found the photograph accidentally. I didn't even know it was there. Why should I? Arabia has been my very dear friend for fifteen years, but in all that time she has had no family, no husband, no son or daughter. Why should I pry into her past? If she wishes to tell it to me, I listen. But I do not pry.'

The courteous voice indicated that the conversation was finished. Mr. Mullins's round rear protruded apologetically from the window as he leaned over to shift a Sheraton tea chest. When he had completed that task his face was a little pinker, but still bland and innocent. Yet Cressida knew that he had lied to her. He had meant her to find the photograph and deduce from it what she

145

could. He was unswervingly loyal to his friend Arabia, but there was something about which he thought Cressida should be warned, some knowledge she should have.

Then, for goodness' sake, why couldn't he say so? Cressida wondered exasperatedly.

'My dear Miss Barclay, you polished that silver punch bowl so well that I sold it half an hour ago. To an American. She intends to use it for flower arrangements, which is perhaps better than filling it with rye whisky or whatever it is that Americans drink. Now, perhaps if you could do the same with this tea service. It's Victorian, but very good. A little too ornate for your taste? What about this George the Third piece? Ah, I can see you like the porcelain best. What do you think of these Dresden candlesticks? You see, they have the same cupid design as the mirror you cleaned the other day.'

Cressida remembered Jeremy's voice, 'What a charming little upside-down face,' and a vague stirring of enchantment died within her almost before it had been born. Too many dreary things had happened since then. Jeremy was tainted more than anyone by the mystery and the macabre happenings. Why was *nobody* frank with her?

She refused to be lured by Mr. Mullins's persuasive voice which told her to ignore the secrets which Arabia did not want known. How could she ignore them when printed indelibly on her mind was the picture of Larry's tombstone, mist-coloured and sad, denying in the sparsity of its information his association with Lucy. Denying his smiling happiness as he held her, a dainty and

146

composed bride, on his arm.

When Cressida got home that night her room was full of mist. She had begun to take the precaution of locking the door, thinking at last to keep out the mischievous person who played tricks on her, but the window was open six inches at the bottom, and it was through there that the mist had seeped. Hadn't she shut the window that morning? She was almost sure she had. Facing directly over the street as it did, the fear of burglars alone made her exercise care. Perhaps she had forgotten it this morning. Anyway, there it was open, and her room full of the damp and chilly mist.

She hastily pushed it down, drew the curtains and switched on the lights.

And then she saw Mimosa.

He was crouched on the carpet in a stiff unnatural position. His eyes were dull, and, lacking his usual slightly elephantine playfulness, he made no sign that he was aware of Cressida's presence.

Cressida knelt beside him. A sudden frightening knowledge seized her. She sprang up and ran to the door.

'Dawson!' she called. She was half-way up the stairs, still calling Dawson frantically, when Mrs. Stanhope, a little white-faced figure obviously full of apprehension, appeared out of her room.

'What is it?' she whispered. 'Dawson isn't home yet. Miss Barclay, surely someone—' Her fear and her throat affliction combined to make the rest of her words inaudible. She wrote frantically on her pad, 'Did someone attack you in the fog?'

Cressida brushed away the writing pad,

147

impatient with Mrs. Stanhope's obsession about the dangers of the streets.

'It's Mimosa, Mr. Winter's cat. He's in my room and he's sick. I think—' There was the sound of the front door opening. 'Oh, there's Dawson now. Dawson, please'—she was running down the stairs again, appealing to the gangling boy whose hair and face gleamed wet with mist—'you must give Mimosa a dose of whatever you gave your mother last night. I think he's been poisoned.'

Dawson gave her a suddenly sharp look, which combined surprise and a boyish satisfaction that his skill was being appealed to.

'I thought you didn't believe Ma had been poisoned.'

'I still don't, but there's something very much wrong with Mimosa. Come and look at him.'

'Shouldn't you tell his owner?' Dawson commented.

'I will, but I haven't had time. You're the expert on medicines.' Dawson went into her room and took a look at Mimosa, crouched in his petrified misery.

'Looks bad,' he said. 'I'll take him upstairs. Ma will help me.'

Thankful to leave Mimosa in expert hands—why was she suddenly so sure that they were expert?—Cressida flew down the stairs to Jeremy's basement.

She knocked, but there was no answer. Now wasn't that just like Jeremy to be off on some light-hearted business of his own while his precious cat was being poisoned. Oh dear, could Dawson handle him, or should she have instantly gone out to find a vet? She ran upstairs again, only to encounter Arabia, who was just returning from some excursion, and who was muffled in a voluminous but very shabby beaver coat.

'Cressida, my dear!' Her rich voice was like warmth and sunshine. 'You're out of breath! Are you running away from Mr. Winter? I always suspected he could be quite a naughty boy.'

'He isn't in, and his cat is sick,' Cressida answered breathlessly. 'Oh, I do hope Dawson can cure it.'

'So do I, poor creature. Has it eaten something strange, too?'

Was that a sly significant look Arabia was giving her out of her hooded eyes?

'I don't know what has happened to it, nor how it got into my room. Too many things have happened,' she added.

Arabia patted her hand. 'My dear, that makes life exciting. As long as they are pleasant things. But even if they are unpleasant, it's so much better than being bored. Don't you agree? Anyway, I know one person who will be very happy if that horrid cat Mimosa is out of the way.'

'Who?' Cressida asked involuntarily.

'Ahmed, of course. He detests the animal. Poor sweet, he comes over in a cold sweat the moment Mimosa's whisker comes round the door. Now, wait a moment. Can a bird come over in a cold sweat? I doubt that. It would make their feathers stick, and they couldn't fly away from the danger that threatened. Stop me, my sweet, if I'm talking nonsense.' Arabia's great warm smile flashed out. She began to sing, '*Oh, for the wings, for the wings of a dove; far away, far away would I fly . . .'* as she climbed the stairs. She disappeared into her room, and her penetrating voice sounded, 'My sweet Ahmed, your enemy is laid low. The great sunflower is vanquished!' And then there began an excited squawking and scuffling as she teased Ahmed and threw him in the air.

It was a game to her, Cressida thought. She didn't care in the least that Mimosa, Jeremy's greatly valued cat, might be dying. It might even be that she had intended him to die, because he upset and angered her precious parrot. It might be that she had deliberately pushed him through the open window into Cressida's room to die there . . .

Mrs. Stanhope appeared at the open door of her room and beckoned violently to Cressida. Cressida went slowly, knowing that Arabia's display of callousness would inevitably be interpreted by Mrs. Stanhope as guilt.

'She's crazy!' she whispered excitedly. 'Do you hear her?'

'She's—high-spirited,' Cressida said lamely.

'But to be so pleased!' The eyes behind the glasses were shocked and enormous. Then Mrs. Stanhope wrote busily, 'Dawson has given the cat an antidote. He seems better.'

At that moment Dawson himself appeared, flushed and triumphant.

'He's been poisoned or doped, I'd say. But I think I've fixed him.'

'Oh, Dawson, you are clever,' Cressida said gratefully.

'That was simple enough, Miss Barclay. Ma held him.'

Mrs. Stanhope wrote, 'I intend that Dawson should study medicine later. He has a natural ability.'

Dawson, the prodigy, said confusedly, 'Aw, Ma, you're nuts. I'm going to be a chemist. Would you like to take the cat down, Miss Barclay? If he's kept warm he'll be all right. You ought to tell Mr. Winter what's happened.'

And that brought the nightmare back, the perplexing question as to what had happened to Mimosa, and how he had got into her room. As if she had been meant to find him dead on her floor...

Her question wasn't answered by Arabia's rich carrying voice singing, '*Forever at rest ... forever ... at ... rest...*'

Or was it? Mrs. Stanhope thought it was. She raised expressive eyes. Dawson muttered again, 'Mr. Winter ought to know. Everyone ought to know,' and went for Mimosa, who was now wrapped in a towel, and laid him in Cressida's arms.

Without another word Cressida turned and went slowly down the stairs with her burden. It was so utterly repugnant to her to think what they were thinking. Last night she had angrily refused to believe them at all. But now...

No, it wasn't possible. Arabia with her warm smile, her kindness, her unpredictable generous heart...

She had meant to take Mimosa back to her room, but he would probably be happier in his own familiar surroundings. If Jeremy had gone out leaving his door unlocked she would take the cat in and leave him beside the embers of the fire.

Surely enough, the door was unlocked. Cressida opened it softly and stood in the darkness of the room. It smelt of tobacco smoke and the stuff Jeremy mixed his paints with, and another more pungent smell—what was it?

Burnt milk, she thought, and at the same moment a voice came out of the shadows.

'What are you doing with my cat?'

CHAPTER THIRTEEN

She couldn't see a thing. She groped for a light switch, but could not find one.

'What are you doing here in the dark?' she demanded suspiciously. 'Why didn't you answer when I knocked?'

'I didn't hear you knock. I was asleep. You woke me just now as you opened the door.'

'Sleeping!' Her voice was full of scorn. 'While someone was quietly trying to kill your cat.'

'Mimosa!' There was a sound of blankets thrown back, and his voice came angrily, incredulously. 'Who the devil would do that? The light switch is the other side of the door. Don't come near me, I've got 'flu. Quickly, put the light on and let me look at Mimosa.'

Cressida at last found the switch and light flooded the now familiar, long, low-ceilinged room with its bright slashes of paint on the walls, and its pictures and rugs—and the divan bed in the corner, where a very irate young man with crazily disordered hair sat upright and glared.

'He's all right now,' Cressida said placatingly.

'Dawson gave him something. Dawson, I might say, is very clever with emetics, even though he looks slightly like a half-wit.'

'Probably enjoys it,' Jeremy muttered. 'Put Mimosa here. Where did you find him? Why wasn't I told? And don't come near me, I said. I'm a mass of germs.'

He began to fondle and examine the cat anxiously. Mimosa responded with an irritated protest, and evading Jeremy's hands settled down at the foot of the bed.

'He seems all right. A bit limp.' Jeremy was plainly relieved. 'Where's your tongue? Can't you tell me what happened?'

'I'm trying to,' Cressida said patiently. 'I found Mimosa in my room. I had left my door locked, but he had got in through the window, which I was sure I hadn't left open. I don't know why he had got into my room, unless he thought that was a nice place to die. Anyway, I rushed out for Dawson because I knew he was good with first-aid. He was just coming in, fortunately, and Arabia came in a moment after. Mrs. Stanhope was home, but I don't know about Miss Glory and Mr. Moretti. I thought you were out because you didn't answer when I knocked, but now you say you were asleep.'

'I was.'

'Arabia told Ahmed it would be a cause for celebration if Mimosa, his great enemy, were dead, but by that time Dawson's cure had been effective, and Mimosa was reviving. Mrs. Stanhope said Dawson ought to be a doctor, and Dawson said everyone ought to know what happened in this house, and then I brought

153

Mimosa down to you. That's all.'

'Enough, I should think,' said Jeremy. His eyes were burning fiercely.

'I'm sorry you are ill,' Cressida said politely.

'That's not the point. I may be dying, but it's from a purely innocent germ I picked up all by myself, whereas—'

'You're just like Tom,' Cressida interrupted. 'He always thinks he's dying when he's ill.'

'Don't compare me to Tom,' Jeremy said bad-temperedly. 'I don't suppose I resemble him in the slightest degree. And take your hand off my head.'

He moved away irritably as Cressida laid her hand on his forehead.

She smiled in gentle amusement and said, 'I think you're getting better. Why didn't you tell me you were ill?'

'Because I didn't want you down here playing Florence Nightingale,' he said snappily. 'It's not only that I don't trust your nursing. You bring too many complications with you. Look at you! Falls down steps, locked doors, death notices, imaginary poisonings—'

'Imaginary!' Cressida said indignantly. 'When I've just helped to save Mimosa's life.'

'He has nine,' Jeremy, who now seemed to have ceased worrying about Mimosa, said, 'I should think he had just picked up a bit of tainted fish. He's a frightful glutton.'

'Then how did he get in my room?'

'You said your window was open, didn't you?'

'But I'm sure I wouldn't leave it open in a fog like this.'

'Far be it from me to contradict,' said Jeremy,

154

'but so far Miss Barclay hasn't impressed me with the methodical side of her nature.'

'You've burnt the milk yourself,' Cressida flashed. 'I can smell it.'

'A person with a high temperature is entitled to a little absent-mindedness,' said Jeremy, lying down and hunching the blankets over his shoulders.

'Oh, I'm so sorry.' Cressida was suddenly contrite. 'I'll get you something to eat. Are you awfully hungry?'

'Not hungry enough for your cooking.'

'You wait and see,' Cressida said amiably. 'I'll make you Tom's speciality when he's feeling off colour.'

'I don't want Tom's anything!' Jeremy shouted, sitting upright. 'I only want you to get out of this room. You with all your melodrama, and now your faithful Tom as well. Oh, you bore me beyond endurance. Why don't you go home to your so precious Tom?'

'But, Jeremy—'

'Don't "but" me in that innocent voice. Go home where you're safe—from all but Tom, that is.'

'Safe?' echoed Cressida.

'Well, what are you doing here?' His voice was harsh. 'You're looking for a dead girl who didn't die, and a grave that doesn't exist.'

'But I found a grave,' Cressida said quietly. 'I found the grave of Lucy's husband Larry. And if you're looking for the entry of Lucy's death again, you must look under the name of Meredith, because that was her name when she died.'

He looked at her, his eyes brilliant with fever,

155

his cheeks shadowed.

'For some reason Arabia won't tell me about that,' Cressida went on. 'She's suddenly putting Lucy right out of her mind, almost as if she had never existed. She's even dismantling that room and shutting it up.'

'Why?' Jeremy asked.

'I don't know. I think I found out more than she wanted me to know. Apparently there was to be a baby that was never born. Oh, it's all so pathetic. I'm very happy to help her try to forget the whole story.'

'But there is still no grave,' Jeremy said, more to himself than to Cressida. 'Unless—'

'Unless what?'

'Unless it's in this house.'

Cressida came quickly and knelt at his bedside. 'What makes you say that?' Her voice was a whisper of horror.

He had instantly regretted his words. He said lightly, 'I'm beginning to imagine things, too.'

'You've no idea how awful it was at the cemetery today, in the mist, with only those few words on Larry's tombstone—beloved son of—no mention of his wife. And he must have loved her. He must have. She was so gay and pretty, and there are all those happy paragraphs in her diary about Larry and flowers and dances. And now all that's left is that single tombstone.' Cressida was crying, the tears running heedlessly down her cheeks.

'Fine way this is to cheer me up,' Jeremy grumbled. 'First Mimosa, then you.' His hand rested for one instant on her hair, then he took it quickly away. 'I'm sorry I was in such a lousy

156

temper. I'll be better tomorrow.'

'Don't—take your hand away.'

'If you're pretending it is Tom's—'

'Actually I wasn't. Jeremy, Arabia shutting that room—it's as if she's at last shutting the coffin. Oh, where is Mimosa's last strip cartoon? For goodness' sake let me cheer myself up. Is it over here?'

But as she went she had to pass the easel, and on it was her own half-finished portrait. She looked at the slender girl with the fly-away hair, the too-wide eyes, the just-beginning smile.

'I look as if I'm listening to a fairy story,' she said involuntarily.

'So you always are.' His voice had got back its dry mocking quality. 'And it's not Lucy's. Or Tom's. It's mine. And you don't listen to it, anyway. You listen to all the other voices that get in the way.'

She looked at him wordlessly. He suddenly waved his long hand in angry impatience.

'Forget it. I'm ill. I'm delirious. Go and get me something to eat before I die.'

'An omelet,' said Cressida happily. 'I can really make very good ones.'

'And tomorrow,' said Jeremy, 'there is something you have to do.'

'What's that?'

'You have to tell Arabia everything that has happened.'

'But she knows. She knows Mrs. Stanhope thinks she was poisoned, and then Mimosa tonight.'

'Does she know you were locked in Lucy's room the other night? Or about the death notice

157

you got?'

'Or that someone tore my notes up,' Cressida added. 'No. I haven't told her those things.'

'Then you must.'

'But if they were her own idea of a joke—she has a very extraordinary sense of humour, Jeremy—it might embarrass her—'

'Embarrass her or not, tell them to her. Tomorrow. And also tomorrow remind me to send you red roses.'

'Red roses!'

'For the illustration I told you about. I want you to be holding them. Don't look so startled. You will have time to pose for me, won't you?'

Cressida tried to shake off her absurd feeling of apprehension, not because Jeremy planned to send her red roses, but because she was to get red roses in this house. This significant house.

'Tom said I ought to be paid.' She was speaking to fill in the silence, to shut out her ridiculous and unfounded apprehension. She wasn't aware of what she had said, but her remark had successfully destroyed the brief truce, and Jeremy was shouting.

'I'll pay you the usual model's fees, and Tom can write them down in neat figures and tot them up and you can both have fun spending them. All I ask in the meantime is that Tom keeps his smug fingers out of my business.'

CHAPTER FOURTEEN

The roses were in Cressida's room the next evening—two dozen long-stemmed, dark-red beauties wrapped in cellophane. Her first reaction was one of pleasure. How very extravagant of Jeremy to buy such exquisite ones. That morning she had slept late, and there had been time only to ascertain that Jeremy was almost completely recovered from his attack of 'flu before rushing off to work. She had seen no one else except Miss Glory, who had clattered in and out in a great hurry, flinging over her shoulder in her flat humourless voice, 'That old woman, she'll drive me crazy. Who's to eat all that stuff tonight? You'd think it was baked meats for a funeral feast.'

There had been no opportunity to obey Jeremy's injunction to tell Arabia about all the odd things that had happened, even supposing Arabia, to whom the story of Lucy was now a closed book, would have listened.

Was the old lady perhaps a schizophrenic? It was beginning to seem very like it.

But there was no time now to worry about that because the house was unexpectedly full of gaiety. All the lights were on. The large glittering chandelier in the hall blazed, and from the open double doors of the ballroom, cleared of Miss Glory's meagre possessions, the parquet floor shone glossily; there were large bowls of flowers, and someone was picking out a dance tune on the piano.

Cressida had a moment of illusion when it seemed to her that the house was waiting for crowds of Lucy's gay, noisy and very young friends to come bursting in. And for Lucy herself to come running down the marble staircase, her skirts flying, her feet swift and excited.

She knew in her heart that this was the illusion Arabia was creating for herself, even though she said stubbornly that the story of Lucy was finished. The story was unfinished until Arabia's own death. The leading part had merely been transferred to Cressida herself, and it was because of Arabia's strange, compelling spell over her that she was willingly playing the part.

She would put on her prettiest dress and wear one of Jeremy's roses. The rest would remain fresh in water until tomorrow, when she would keep her part of the bargain by sitting for him so that he could complete his picture.

Who had used to send Lucy red roses?

Cressida, like Arabia, decided briskly to dismiss Lucy from her mind, temporarily at least, and ran down the steep stairs to the basement to see how Jeremy was, and to say her polite thank you for the roses which, exquisite as they were, were only part of a business deal.

At her knock he came to the door; and almost before Cressida could observe that he was fully dressed and looked well though still pale, Mimosa bounded past her legs and up the stairs, a blond torpedo.

'Nothing much wrong with him,' she commented.

'He's in one of his moods,' Jeremy said. 'Quite uncontrollable. I told him he was going to Paris.'

'Is he?'

'Only on paper. Unless you come, too. No, don't say it. Tom wouldn't approve. Is the almighty shadow of Tom to hang over us forever?'

'I don't think there's much wrong with you, either,' Cressida said dryly. 'I believe both you and Mimosa have been pretending, to get a little attention.'

'It looks as if you're not lacking for attention yourself.' Jeremy said, looking at the sheaf of roses, still in their cellophane.

'Yes, it really was too extravagant of you. I hope the author or the magazine pays for these. I know they don't mean a thing beyond business, but they really are beautiful.'

'Hang on a moment!' Jeremy's mobile eyebrow was rising towards his hair again. His face was both amused and curiously distressed. 'You're saying thank you to the wrong person. I haven't sent you any roses. Mine were ordered for tomorrow, and I'm afraid only a meagre dozen. Tom has rather spread himself. Is this a bribe, do you think or is he naturally inclined to buy large sheafs of out-of-season flowers?'

'No, of course he isn't. He would spend his money to better purpose.' Cressida's voice was suddenly sharp, because she was realising, guiltily, that for the first time there had been no letter from Tom, and she hadn't even missed it. 'These can't be from Tom,' she added definitely. 'Unless he has suddenly gone out of his mind.' She began tearing at the cellophane covering the flowers, in her attempt to get at the enclosed card. 'Once he sent me a gardenia,' she said. 'That was to wear at the annual dinner of his firm, and we had just

161

become engaged. He thought that was very festive. Oh-h-h ...' The card trembled in her sudden nerveless fingers. Jeremy caught it as she was going to drop it.

It was a black-bordered square, and it simply said, 'In Memoriam.'

The house was suddenly hostile. Something cold and frightening in it had moved closer. It was no use to look at the bright lights or listen to the tripping waltz that was now coming from the ballroom, or even to notice the faint savoury smells that occasionally wafted through the air. There was to be a ghost at the feast after all, the ghost of a young, gay and foolish girl who had once loved red roses.

'Did you tell Arabia what I told you to?' Jeremy was demanding sternly.

'No, I haven't. I haven't had time. This morning she wasn't up when I left, and tonight—how can I tonight?'

'Tonight may be the very time.' But now Jeremy was turning away and refusing to explain his muttered words. 'Unless you'd like to go now, while the going's good.'

'Go!' Cressida repeated stupidly.

'To Euston or Paddington or wherever you catch your train home to Tom. I'll see you there if you can pack quickly.'

'*Now!*' said Cressida. 'But you're mad! How can I leave before the party has even started? Why, it's my party!'

Jeremy looked at her with his cryptic gaze.

'I suppose I couldn't expect you to disappoint the old lady. In spite of what she may be happy to do to you. Well, don't blame me if your soft heart

162

gets you into trouble. Go and dress up and be Lucy for them. Satisfy them once more. And then perhaps we'll be able to lay those damned roses on *your* grave.'

'Jeremy!' She was gripping his arm. 'You keep saying them! Who is them?'

'I wish I knew,' he said softly. 'I wish I knew.'

★ ★ ★

Only Miss Glory knew anything about the roses, and she just said that she had taken them from the messenger boy at the door. There was no florist's name on the card.

'My word, he must think a lot of you,' she said to Cressida. 'They'd cost a fortune this time of the year. Look at those stems.'

'But I don't know who sent them.'

Miss Glory did not believe her. She winked and looked coy, and said, 'Lucky girl. Have you so many admirers? And all of them wealthy?' and then whisked away to the kitchen to see to the dinner.

Wealthy? Was that the clue? Arabia was the only wealthy person in this house. Were the roses her final gesture of farewell to Lucy, and of welcome to Cressida, the new Lucy? Jeremy thought so, only Jeremy seemed to think there was something more sinister than a poignant gesture of farewell in this particular bouquet. Why did he suddenly think that?

There was no time to talk about them now. Everyone was dressing for dinner and she would be late. Some time this evening she had to get Arabia by herself and insist on her being honest.

163

There was so much to be explained. The roses, nostalgic reminders of Lucy, were surely the climax.

Cressida, refusing to be perturbed by the disturbing gift, wore one of the roses in the bosom of her dress, and went out gaily to the party.

The dinner table was laid in the curve of the tall ballroom windows. Half an hour later they were all seated round it. Miss Glory, looking more than ever like a flat figure cut out of cardboard, in a narrow black dress with a virginal string of pearls round her thin neck, bustled backwards and forwards from the kitchen with food. Mr. Moretti, explaining that he had to leave early to go to his night-club, wore a dinner jacket, but Mrs. Stanhope and Dawson could not approach this grandeur. Mrs. Stanhope looked more inconspicuous and owl-like than ever in grey, and Dawson wore the tweed jacket, presumably his only respectable garment, which he wore every day to work.

It was Arabia, of course, who stole the show. She must have put on every jewel she possessed, and she glittered like a Burmese temple god. Her taste had obviously never been for inconspicuous jewellery. She liked large opulent stones in heavy settings. Most of them were only semi-precious, and on a second look Cressida realised that she was not worth the fortune she would seem to be. Garnets were not rubies, nor turquoises emeralds. Indeed, some of the large stones glittering on her bosom or her fingers may simply have been glass, but that did not take away her appearance of fabulous richness.

Dawson, at least, was hypnotised by her, and

164

could not take his eyes from her sparkling figure. Arabia was fully aware of his fascination, and of being the focal point of the party. It was the kind of attention she loved, and to which she responded in her inimitable way.

'Yes, look at me,' she chuckled. 'You'll never have another landlady who looks like this. Oh, I don't say that some of them don't have fortunes hidden away in teapots, probably much larger ones than mine, but they come out looking about as exciting as pieces of darning wool. Now me, I adore looking opulent. Do I look opulent tonight? Tell me, boy, do I?'

She chucked Dawson beneath his sharp chin, and the embarrassed colour flowed into his cheeks.

'You look wonderful, Mrs. Bolton,' he muttered.

Well pleased, for, although she might despise Dawson as a weedy and singularly unattractive youth, she never failed to respond to a compliment, Arabia proceeded to enlarge on the subject.

'It was really my old friend, the sheik, who taught me not to be miserly about my appearance. He adored magnificence, and secretly I always had, too. So I blossomed in the desert. Ah, how I blossomed! Jeremy, stop raising your eyebrows! You think I'm romancing?'

'Most entertainingly,' said Jeremy.

Arabia rapped the table.

'Naughty boy! All I tell you is true. True! Look at this ring. It was a present from an Indian rajah. And this brooch my second husband gave me on our tenth wedding anniversary. My ear-rings my third husband bought me in Peking after we had travelled by the old silk route into China. And this adorable necklace was the dear sheik's gift. Yes, I know it is a little vulgar and showy, but opulence, opulence is all! I remember that jewel shop in Baghdad—But you are all laughing at me! A foolish bedizened old woman!'

Her gaze swept the table challengingly. Mr. Moretti got swiftly to his feet and made a small graceful bow.

'Madam, you are magnificent. You look like a heathen goddess.'

Arabia smiled with appreciative delight.

'Exactly the kind of thing the sheik used to say. We must dance later. You dance almost as well as a gigolo I once met in Singapore, and that is no small compliment. Ah, life is full of beginnings and endings. And then beginnings again.'

'And the food's getting cold,' Miss Glory said tartly. 'Who, I ask you again, is to carve the duck?'

'In a moment we'll decide that. Let's first pour the wine. Jeremy, fill everyone's glass. And then I have a toast to give you.'

Jeremy obediently filled everyone's glass with the rose-coloured wine, and then Arabia, at the head of the table, stood and raised her glass.

Cressida had a moment's swift apprehension. What was the old lady, glittering and quite quite mad, going to say? Was she going to drink to dead Lucy? Could one raise one's glass and drink to a ghost?

But Arabia's face had grown curiously gentle and happy and almost humble. She said in her warm, husky voice,

166

'To the spring. Let us drink to the return of spring.'

And in that moment all her apparent madness seemed like sanity. She was suddenly the most beautiful person in the room.

After that, the party proceeded as well as any party could with such oddly assorted guests. The food was eaten and the wine drunk, then the table cleared and pushed back and Miss Glory commanded to go to the piano and play a waltz. But Miss Glory, after a few opening bars, suddenly began to sing, ' *'Tis the last rose of summer, blooming alone...*'

'We can't dance to that,' Arabia said impatiently.

Mr. Moretti lifted his slender graceful hand.

'I beg you, dear lady. Just a moment. This is my favourite song.'

Was it imagination that his gaze slid down to the rose at Cressida's breast? Cressida could not be sure. Neither could she be sure that Mrs. Stanhope and Dawson were not suddenly staring pointedly at the flower she had recklessly decided to wear. Arabia, it was certain, was. For the first time she was aware of the nature of Cressida's ornament, and her eyes abruptly took on their hooded secret look.

'A red rose,' she whispered. 'My dear child—'

'*All its lovely companions,*' sang Miss Glory in her thin high voice, '*are faded and gone...*'

'But since you sent then to me—' Cressida began bewilderedly.

'Sent them to you!' Arabia's eyelids lifted momentarily, then dropped once more over her too-revealing eyes. Had that been triumph in them—or fear? 'My dear child, why should I do such a thing? *Her* flowers, when you know that I have decided once and for always to put her out of my mind. Oh, for heaven's sake, Miss Glory, stop that funereal song! This is a party.'

Miss Glory's hands fell with a crash on to the keys. Arabia slipped her arm possessively round Cressida. Her old arrogant head was lifted high. 'If someone,' she began in her rich resonant voice, 'has thought it amusing, or even kind and sentimental, to send Cressida what were once my daughter's favourite flowers, I would like them to know that that kind of thing no longer meets with my approval. I have spent nearly twenty years of my life grieving for my daughter, and that has been long enough. I told you that life is full of beginnings. Tonight you see one more. I have a new daughter, I am a magician, a conjurer. I have brought back the spring. This is the new Cressida Lucy. She is young and gay and very, very kind, and she has charmed away my sorrow.'

She really is mad, Cressida was telling herself. The thin old arm round her waist gripped with surprising tightness, and the hard stones of the ornate bracelets and rings pressed into her flesh. Yet her dominating sensation, as always, was one of helpless admiration and love for the extraordinary, warm-hearted, unpredictable old creature. She could not hurt her. No, no matter what happened, she could not bring back that look of hopeless grief into Arabia's eyes.

'So I'll bore you no more with my tales of Lucy. She is buried now, deep in her grave. She is resigned at last to death.'

It was absurd and melodramatic, and no one

168

was shedding tears for a girl so long dead who no one except her bewitched old mother knew. Yet a curious, hypnotised silence had fallen over the room. When Arabia announced, with a sudden brittle gaiety, that everyone must be kind to Cressida or when she became their new landlady, as she would one day, she might turn them all out and keep only cats, it was almost a relief to hear the tinkle of glass and see that Mrs. Stanhope had spilt wine down the front of her dress.

Arabia gave her great peal of laughter.

'Don't be so nervous, my dear. Cressida, I can assure you, is much too kind-hearted to hurt anyone at all. She won't turn you out.'

Mrs. Stanhope, her face highly flushed, mopped nervously at her dress.

'Dawson bumped me,' she whispered. 'So clumsy.'

Dawson, embarrassed, held his bony elbows closely against his sides. 'Sorry, Ma,' he muttered.

'I must go and change. Excuse me.' The bird-like whispering ceased as Mrs. Stanhope hurried from the room.

And Mr. Moretti waltzed into the middle of the floor, his pale eyes half-closed, his wide smile spreading emptily.

'In five minutes I must leave. Dance with me first, dear lady.'

Miss Glory turned, with enthusiasm, to the piano, and began to play vigorously. Arabia swam, glittering, into Mr. Moretti's arms, and Jeremy who had lounged silently in the background for some time took Cressida's arm and said, 'I think I am strong enough to dance.'

She moved across the floor as if in a dream.

'Jeremy, I think everyone is mad. *Who* sent me the roses?'

'Arabia has periods of convenient amnesia,' he said.

'But why? Why be so absolutely sweet to me, and then behind my back play these horrid unamusing tricks?'

'Because, as I've suggested before, you remind her too much of Lucy. Sometimes she likes this, but occasionally, in little isolated black moments, she hates and resents you because you are alive and Lucy is dead.'

'Jeremy, do you really believe all that?'

He nodded his head, but she could see the disbelief in his eyes. He looked suddenly older, his face all lines and shadows.

'Jeremy, you're not well yet. You shouldn't be here. After all, only yesterday you were running a high temperature.'

He gave her his mocking smile.

'Sweet lady, I would get off my deathbed to look after you.'

'After me! But—then do you think—' The cold was coming nearer again. Everything was menacing—Miss Glory's tripping music, Mr. Moretti's smoothly moving figure, a neat black backdrop for Arabia's glitter, Dawson lounging in the doorway...

'Someone here may not particularly care for the thought of your becoming Arabia's heiress,' Jeremy said in his low casual voice. 'Someone may think you are a usurper.'

'Of course,' Cressida breathed. 'How dumb I am.'

'Beautiful but dumb.'

'But no one here has any claim on Arabia. Lodgers in a house surely do not expect to inherit their landlady's fortune.'

'And what about you?'

'Yes, I know I'm a lodger, but the difference is I don't want this money. I don't *want* to be Arabia's heiress. The thought appals me. But how can I hurt her feelings? It makes her so happy. And I've told you before, I don't need to keep the money.'

'If you live to receive it,' Jeremy commented drily.

'Jeremy, you don't think—you mean that death notice and the in memoriam are serious warnings. But—'

Not heeding the horror in her voice, Jeremy went on calmly,

'Miss Glory has been here the longest. She had endured Arabia's bullying and her eccentric behaviour for several years, and she isn't a servant, mind you. On Arabia's death she would be homeless. Moretti, apart from you, has been here the least time. He seems harmless enough, but he's a type with whom a little extra money would not go amiss. He probably has dreams of opening his own establishment. Do you notice the way Arabia laps up his old-world-courtesy act?'

'He flirts with Miss Glory,' Cressida said breathlessly. 'It could be that the two of them are plotting. All that mournful music he plays could be his perverted sense of humour.'

'That has only started since you came,' Jeremy said.

'Oh! Has it really? Like the—the other things.'

Cressida's fascinated attention was now on Mr.

171

Moretti, with his straw-pale hair, his pink face bent courteously to Arabia, his smooth sophisticated dancing. But Jeremy went on with his calm analysis.

'The Stanhopes have been here three months. The woman is as nervous as a rabbit. She seems scared stiff of Arabia, but she's determined to stay here for some reason. It might only be that Arabia never charges a high rent, or it might be for a much more secret reason. Have you noticed the way Dawson hangs round Arabia, asking to do things for her and acting like a little well-trodden-down worm?'

'But Arabia can't endure him,' Cressida said.

'How true. But what fond mother realises that other people might dislike her precious offspring? It could be that Mrs. Stanhope visualised her son becoming indispensable to a lonely old woman—until you arrived and upset her plans.'

'She told me that day that the room was let! Did she do it deliberately?'

'She could have, indeed. What chance had bespectacled Dawson if he had to compete both with you and the ever-present legend of Lucy?'

'They keep talking of murder,' Cressida whispered. 'But they wouldn't do anything. They wouldn't have the courage for anything but little mean underhand things.'

'And that brings us to me,' Jeremy went on. 'The mysterious dweller in the basement, the sinister kidnapper of pretty girls—no, pretty isn't the word for you—you're credulous and idiotically soft-hearted, and you deserve everything that is going to happen to you, but some day I will get that look of yours on to canvas, that look of listening to fairy stories and songs.'

'Jeremy! We're talking about you! Were you planning to be Arabia's heir, before I arrived? After all, you live in the basement on the idiotic pretext of catching burglars—'

'And I have no money, and I take what I want, unscrupulously, even if it belongs to another man.'

His arms tightened round her. Arabia's voice suddenly boomed across the room.

'Are you two making love? Jeremy, come and dance with me. Vincent has to go now.'

'Yes, I'm devastated,' said Mr. Moretti, in his exaggerated way. He bent to kiss Arabia's hand. 'This has been an enchanting party, dear lady. But now back to the inferno.'

'Where you belong,' Arabia said comfortably. 'He has a slight look of the devil about him, hasn't he? That bleached hair and singed eyebrows. From too much heat, no doubt.'

She gave her rich peal of laughter, and turned tirelessly to Jeremy to begin another dance.

But at that moment Mrs. Stanhope re-entered the room. She had changed from the mousy-grey dress into the equally drab brown wool that she usually wore in the afternoons. Her only concession to the party was a rather girlish locket of seed pearls which was probably one of her few treasures from her youth. She came into the room fingering it in her nervous way, and whispering apologies for her disappearance.

'So clumsy of me with the wine.'

Since no one else spoke and Arabia appeared to be staring at her with her hooded look, as if to mask contempt, Cressida said kindly, 'What a

173

pretty locket.'

Mrs. Stanhope fiddled for her pencil and pad and wrote in her quick, eager way, as if afraid that if she did not hurry she would again be left out of the conversation.

'My mother gave it to me on my eighteenth birthday.'

'How nice,' Cressida murmured.

The party had suddenly gone dead. Mr. Moretti had gone, the music had stopped, and Arabia was full of her hooded contempt for the mousy little woman who was inadvertently getting all the attention, first with the spilled wine and now with her girlish scrap of jewellery.

Mimosa's sudden wail somewhere in the hall was almost as if it had been a rehearsed diversion. There was a pounding and a bumping, and more anguished wails from the cat as apparently he fled down to the basement.

Cressida, who had been nearest to the door, was at the head of the basement stairs first. She didn't know who came after her, but she did wonder fleetingly why, suddenly, only one dim light burned in the hall, at the far end, and the basement stairs were in darkness. Mimosa! Someone was doing something to him! Last night it had been some dubious food, now—what was causing him to squawk like that?

There were confused voices behind her. She groped for the light switch at the head of the stairs. Jeremy's voice called, 'Cressida!' And then, in the darkness, someone bumped into her and she fell.

It was not a bad fall. She had clutched at the stair rail, and that had prevented her from rolling to the bottom of the steep stone steps. She had wrenched her knee slightly, and it felt as if someone had clutched at her throat. And now there were arms about her tightly, and someone was kissing her.

Light flooded on. It was Jeremy who held her, so tightly that she could scarcely breathe. Had he pushed her and then regretted it? The thought flashed through her mind and vanished.

Jeremy's face was too stripped of its mocking mask. It was too thin and anxious, and her lips were still warm from his kiss.

Why had he suddenly kissed her? There was no time to think of that. 'Mimosa!' she said.

'Cressida! Are you all right?' That was Miss Glory's voice from the top of the stairs. It was harsh and hard, as if she had had a very great fright. Looking up Cressida saw Mrs. Stanhope, also, peering fearfully through the big glasses, and a moment later there was Dawson, carrying Mimosa, who struggled violently, but who otherwise appeared safe and unhurt.

There was no sign of Arabia.

Cressida got to her feet. 'I'm all right,' she said, laughing. 'Why are you all looking so worried? I only slipped in the dark. Dawson, is Mimosa all right?'

Jeremy took the cat from Dawson and examined him. Mimosa still struggled wildly, all his claws extended.

'He's only had a fright over something,' he said. 'I wonder what.'

'I can tell you that, Mr. Winter,' Dawson said, and like a conjurer produced from behind his back a flat tin with a string through it. 'This was tied to his tail. He nearly tore me to pieces while I got it off. No wonder he squawked.'

Jeremy's face went black. 'Who did this?' His fierce eyes swept the watching people. But who was there to look at—only Miss Glory who suddenly looked old and angry and incredulous, Mrs. Stanhope who was visibly trembling, and Dawson who had rescued Mimosa at the cost of scratched and bleeding hands.

'It would probably be the kids in the street,' Dawson volunteered. 'I've seen them teasing the cat before. They probably caught him and tied the tin to his tail and then threw him in a window.'

'What window?' Jeremy said unbelievingly.

'It would be mine, the same as yesterday,' Cressida said, scrambling up the stairs. 'Come and see.'

She limped up to her room, followed by the rest. Surely enough her window was open slightly at the bottom and fog seeped in. She knew she had left it shut earlier that evening, but the catch was old and weak, and now it hung crookedly, where it had given way when the window had been pushed up.

'You see,' she said. 'The house has a hoodoo on it. Or this room has.'

Miss Glory suddenly began to laugh in a high-pitched, hysterical way.

'Like hell it has! she exclaimed, and stumbled out of the room, almost as if she were in deadly fear.

'Where's Arabia?' said Jeremy.

'I think she went upstairs,' said Dawson. 'It would be the kids in the street who did that to Mimosa, Mr. Winter. They'd think it would be a

176

joke to spoil the party.'

'You're sure you didn't do it yourself,' Jeremy demanded.

Dawson's face went long and hurt. His mother scribbled rapidly, 'Dawson loves animals. He saved Mimosa's life yesterday.'

Dawson nodded mutely. 'Mind you, it might only have been a bit of tainted fish he'd had. And those kids might have done that, too.'

That, indeed, seemed the most likely explanation of all.

But it didn't explain why Arabia had so suddenly disappeared, nor why, when they went up to see what she was doing, she had locked her door and refused to come out.

CHAPTER FIFTEEN

Cressida was worried about her. The old lady had been enjoying the party so much, and although she was inclined to sudden changes of mood, Mimosa's unfortunate contretemps surely could not so abruptly have plunged her from gaiety into gloom.

There was another thought that niggled at Cressida. Her fall on the stairs had been caused by someone bumping into her, which could have been accidental, but on the other hand it could have been deliberate. It was unlikely that such a fall would have killed her, but she could have been severely hurt. The accident could have been in a line with the other stupid but unpleasant things that had happened, all of them harmless, but with their discomforting flavour of the diabolic. As if their perpetrator had more than a dash of the sinister.

Was Arabia the guilty person? Beneath her warmth and charm did she conceal a virulent hate for all young and pretty girls who reminded her of her dead daughter? Had Cressida been lured into a snare, to be played with first, and then—

No, all that conjecture was absurd. Now that the house was quiet and dark, with the ballroom once more Miss Glory's domain (Cressida had helped her to carry out the bowls of flowers and put her narrow bed back into its place), Cressida went up the stairs and tapped again on Arabia's door.

For a long time there was no answer. Mrs. Stanhope, wrapped in a cotton housecoat that had no colour at all, appeared down the passage, tiptoeing with exaggerated caution, and wrote busily on her everlasting pad, 'She won't see anyone when she's in that mood. You are better to leave her alone.'

Her large, solemn, spectacled eyes indicated that Arabia was mad. Dawson, the inevitable shadow, nodded in the background. Cressida pressed her fingers to her temples. She was very tired. Her knee throbbed a little from her fall, and the delayed shock, or only half-acknowledged fear or apprehension, gave her a feeling of complete exhaustion. Her head was full of kaleidoscopic pictures and voices—Arabia waltzing with her elderly dignity in the too rich, too formal dress (*she's mad, she's crazy* ...); Mr. Moretti bending over her hand with his suave courtly gesture, his eyes hidden behind their colourless lashes (*the*

178

poor old thing is crazy, but wealthy, wealthy ...);
Arabia giving her great shout of laughter as she
related one of her exaggerated stories (*no one but
an eccentric would tell stories like that* ...); Mrs.
Stanhope standing mousy and embarrassed with
the wine spilt down her frock; Jeremy's teasing
voice suggesting that one person there might be
an unscrupulous robber, a more than sinister
prankster (*an old crazy woman could be easy prey
*...); Miss Glory's thin high voice singing, '*All her
lovely companions are faded and gone*'; and Arabia's
eyes suddenly on the rose at Cressida's breast ...
And always the glitter, the glitter of the incredible
old lady who suddenly, after twenty years of
faithful mourning for her adored daughter, had
announced that she had forgotten the past...

Suddenly there was a shuffling within Arabia's
room, and the old lady's voice, whispered and
cautious, came hissingly through the door.

'Who is it?'

'It's me Cressida. Won't you let me come in?'

'No, dear, no. Go away, I beg you. Go away.'

'You mean right away? Out of this house?'
Cressida was bewildered.

'That would be better,' came the voice from
within. There was more shuffling, and a sudden
startled squawk from Ahmed, as if he had been
squeezed or trodden on.

'But, Arabia!' Cressida beat softly on the door
with her clenched fist. 'You can't behave like this,
after that lovely party. Why have you locked your
door?'

'Because I have been too gullible. Ah, how
could I have been so gullible! What would the
sheik have thought of me? Oh, stupid old woman

that I am?'

'Arabia, darling! Stop being so melodramatic and open your door.'

'I daren't, my dear. I daren't.'

She really was mad. Cressida could visualise her inside the fantastic, untidy room, a glittering and dishevelled figure, crouching uncertainly against the door, listening—for what imagined danger?

'Then it really is you who have been doing all those peculiar things?' Cressida's voice begged for a denial.

'Everything is my fault. You should never have come here. The house is tainted.' The rich, vital voice was full of despair, the voice of a tragedienne, full of conviction that her act was real. 'But Cressida, are you listening?'

'Yes, I'm listening.'

'Do you really love me? Just a little? Just for what I am, a stupid old woman who likes colour and life and opulence, and who means to be kind?'

Cressida felt tears burning her eyelids. She longed to put a protecting arm round the tired old body weighed down with its opulence, and to bring back the humour and sparkle to the magnificent eyes. Who could not love Arabia for her very warm-hearted, impulsive craziness?

'Of course! Of course I do!' she answered.

There was an audible sigh from within. Arabia's voice was little more than a whisper.

'Then it will be worth it, after all.'

*　　　*　　　*

At the moment, later in the night, that Cressida

suddenly remembered Jeremy's unexpected kiss after her fall—and it had certainly not been the kiss one would give a hurt child—she heard the sound outside her door.

The luminous face of her clock showed one o'clock, more than three hours since the party had broken up. Without allowing herself time to be afraid, she got out of bed, wrapped her dressing-gown round her, and opened her door so quickly that the person leaning against it half fell into her room.

She gave a stifled cry and looked into the smiling and unrepentant face of Jeremy.

'What on earth—' she began.

He had a sketching board in his hand. His face was drawn and lined with weariness, his hair a tousled mass. At his feet Mimosa stretched, sound asleep.

'Mimosa and I are completing our trip to Paris,' he explained. 'We're just in the act of descending the Eiffel Tower. Mimosa is a little nervous, but I find the atmosphere quite irresistible.'

His sparkling eyes looked into hers. It was as if—no, he couldn't be so confident—that kiss begun on the stairs were to be completed here and now.

'But why here?' she exclaimed. 'In this draughty cold hall and you scarcely out of bed after 'flu. And it's long past midnight. Is everyone in this house mad?'

'No,' he said slowly. 'Only cautious.'

'Jeremy—' Her eyes questioned him.

'Last night you looked after me. Tonight I look after you.'

181

'You're not spending the night out here! Not just because of a few jokes being played on me.'

'Your sense of humour is keener than Mimosa's. He didn't think that tin on his tail was particularly funny.'

'Then you don't think that children in the street—'

'I haven't noticed any children in this street. Have you? Particularly not ones who would still be up and playing outside at ten o'clock on a dark, foggy night.'

Cressida met his eyes.

'I'm not really as dumb as you think. There are just—some things—that I haven't let myself believe.'

'So there are,' said Jeremy soothingly. 'And one is that I actually like working here late at night. I'm getting on very well, so please don't disturb me again. Go back to bed and get some sleep.'

'If you must do this—wouldn't you be more comfortable in my living-room?'

His eyebrow went up.

'Would Tom approve?'

'Oh, bother Tom!'

He made no comment, but the smile spread from his lips into his eyes. He followed her into the room and spread his board on the table. Then he picked up Mimosa, who obligingly allowed himself to be posed on the table beside the bowl of roses.

'Excellent,' he said. 'Now we'll complete our descent of the Eiffel Tower and dine at Fouquets. You go back to bed. This has nothing to do with you.'

Cressida yawned. 'I'm too sleepy to worry any

more. And, anyway, Arabia admitted all those things tonight. So there's no mystery left. I suppose I should hate her, an eccentric twisted old woman. But I don't. I still think she's wonderful and I intend to stay and look after her, and I couldn't be less interested in her money, even if she had any, which I doubt. Most of her jewels are false. They must be, or she would keep them in a vault.'

'Go to sleep,' said Jeremy. 'Mimosa and I may take you to Paris with us next time.'

Cressida, in the next room, climbed tiredly into bed.

'Not the Eiffel Tower. Too exhausting,' she murmured.

'No, the Bois de Boulogne, and Fontainbleau. In the spring. A room that looks over the Seine and Notre Dame. Tulips and real mimosa. Coffee and croissants, and the shops in the Rue de la Paix. The gardens of the Tuileries, or perhaps, like Mimosa, you prefer the fountains in the Place de la Concorde?'

But Cressida, smiling faintly, was asleep.

*　　　*　　　*

Upstairs Arabia, although she lay in her bed with Ahmed perched in his usual place on the bedpost, was not asleep. She knew that she would not sleep that night. The only thing was to pass the hours of darkness as comfortably as possible. If she kept all the lights burning, both in her bedroom and in the living-room, a little of her confidence and courage would return. She would not be just a frail old woman trembling in the dark, ashamed of her cowardice.

Ahmed did not like the lights and ruffled his feathers resentfully. In the living-room the several lamps in their brightly-coloured, pleated and tasselled shades glowed with a festive air. In their gaiety they were not unlike the great handfuls of jewels which Arabia had flung down on to her dressing-table.

She had always loved colour and glitter. Even in her youth, when her face and body were magnificent enough to need no decoration, she had liked coloured scarves and heavy jewellery. In later years Lucy had used to laugh at her and begged her to leave off one bracelet or one rope of pearls. These were the young and tender spring days when Lucy still laughed.

Now she could cover all her wrinkles and sagging flesh, weigh herself down with glittering stones, produce a brave defiance against the ravages of age, and there was no one to laugh at her, tolerantly or otherwise.

But she was wrong. There was Cressida now. Cressida brought warmth into her heart again, she was lovely and gay and kind and sincere. Oh, there was no doubting her sincerity. So the game was worth playing in spite of everything. She would play it to the end.

Whatever the end was ... Was that a sound she heard? A creeping, a whispered voice in the next room? Arabia started up. She listened intently. No, there was nothing. The lights flooded into every corner. There were no shadows.

Oh, it was too bad the party had been spoilt tonight, too bad! It had been such a gay and happy party. One had thought all the ghosts had been laid.

But now she knew they were never to be laid...

CHAPTER SIXTEEN

Cressida awakened to find Miss Glory standing over her with her early-morning tea.

'Does Mr. Winter want tea, too?' she asked in her flat voice.

Cressida started up, suddenly wanting to laugh. The room was full of grey, foggy light, and Miss Glory's face looked longer and more lacking in humour than ever, but still laughter, like sunlight, bubbled up inside her.

'Is he still out there?' she asked.

'He's asleep in the chair.'

'Oh, poor Jeremy! He had an absurd idea last night that I needed a watch-dog.'

She expected Miss Glory to be completely sceptical of this explanation, and the coy, girlish look which Mr. Moretti aroused in her to come over her face. Surprisingly enough, Miss Glory remained quite solemn.

'He may have been right, at that,' she said, and flapped off to the door.

Presently she came back and put a cup and saucer down clatteringly on the table in the other room. The noise must have woken Jeremy, for Miss Glory said, 'And about time, too. It's after eight o'clock,' as if Jeremy's presence there were the most natural thing in the world.

Jeremy appeared briefly at Cressida's door.

'I'm terribly sorry, I went to sleep. I should

have been out of here before daylight.'

'I shouldn't think in this house it matters what happens,' Cressida said. She still felt gay and light-hearted, last night's events a mere fantasy that did not exist by daylight.

'Nothing did happen,' Jeremy said, somewhat cryptically. 'There's a letter from Tom. Do you want it now?'

'Not until after breakfast.'

'Wise girl. Save your strength.'

'What for?'

'To say no.'

Cressida knew she should be angry with him—a wakeful night seemed to have increased his impudence—but it was so pleasant to be light-hearted, to forget her fears and perplexities, and behave as if it were quite normal for a young man with a mocking face and dark, untidy hair to be looking in her bedroom door. Last night he had talked of Paris, she remembered. And last night, from fear or relief, or simply the unexpected opportunity, he had kissed her...

'I'm going now,' he said. 'I shall expect you to dinner, and then a sitting for me tonight.'

Tonight—was life going on as normally as that? Cressida thought of Arabia stubbornly locked in her room, of the constant mysterious happenings, of Jeremy's own fears for her safety last night. But, after all, what could happen today? She would be safely working in Mr. Mullins's shop, she would have lunch at the café round the corner, she would not visit churches or cemeteries or do anything at all that may be distressing or unsafe. She would even come home before dark. Today she would leave Lucy's story strictly alone.

Like Arabia, she would play the ostrich game of putting her head in the sand.

That way, what was there to stop her from eating dinner with Jeremy in the basement room that was becoming a familiar refuge?

'All right,' she said. 'I'll come.'

Before she left for work, however, she ran upstairs and tapped at Arabia's door. Arabia surely could not still be indulging in the whim that led her to lock herself in her room.

'Who is it?' Once more there was the cautious query.

'It's Cressida again. Please open the door. I want to say thank you for the lovely party last night.'

'That's all right, my dear. I'm glad you liked it.' The voice was infinitely weary. At last it sounded its seventy-five years and more.

'Arabia, are you ill?'

'No, dear. Only very tired.'

'But why have you locked your door?'

'Because it's safer, of course.' Arabia's voice was suddenly tart, as if she were impatient with the slowness of Cressida's perception.

'Arabia—aren't you imagining something? No one's going to hurt you. After all—'

'You don't know what you're talking about,' the old lady retorted, with something of her former fire and vitality. 'Oh, I hate this house, I hate it! If only I had a camel, sand dunes, the desert wind, oh, I'd ride for dear life ...' Her voice died away as she moved from the door and out of hearing.

Cressida turned away slowly. She encountered Miss Glory with a breakfast tray on the stairs.

'Oh, Miss Glory, what's the matter with Mrs. Bolton?' she cried.

'She's afraid she's going to be poisoned, that's all.' The answer, in Miss Glory's matter-of-fact voice, seemed all the more shocking.

'Poisoned! But that's absurd! Why, she herself—'

'Absurd or not, she makes me sit down and taste everything first,' Miss Glory interrupted. 'It doesn't matter if I die. Frankly, I don't care one way or the other.'

She went on her gloomy way, rapped at the door, called briefly, 'It's me,' and then disappeared through the narrow space of the reluctantly opened door.

The door closed again and Cressida heard the key click in the lock.

Only one other strange thing happened before Cressida left for work. That was the spectacle of Mr. Moretti, in his dressing-gown, appearing in the passage and calling querulously, 'Rosebud! Have you forgotten me this morning? Where are you, Rosebud, my own?'

But Miss Glory was upstairs with Arabia, and out of hearing. The extraordinary thing was that she should have neglected Mr. Moretti for Arabia. On other mornings Mr. Moretti had been attended to first, without fail. Did that mean she was genuinely concerned about Arabia's behaviour, or was it that she was suddenly displeased with her flirtatious suitor? Cressida could not imagine the latter happening. Miss Glory's infatuation had been too deep for displeasure.

No one had mentioned her fall the previous

evening. It came as a surprise when Mr. Mullins asked her why she was limping.

'Oh, was I? I didn't realise. I slipped on the stairs last night and hurt my knee. It's nothing, really.'

'How did you come to slip?' Was Mr. Mullins's voice expressing nothing but polite concern, or did he think it odd and suspicious that she should have had a fall?

Now she was beginning to read significance into the most innocent things. Nothing could be more kind and innocent than Mr. Mullins's bland, pink face and gently concerned eyes.

'We all went out to see what Mimosa was doing, and the lights weren't on, and I slipped,' she said quickly.

Before Mr. Mullins could comment on that statement she said on an impulse, 'Mr. Mullins, do you think Arabia is mad?'

'No,' he said at once.

'But you don't know all the odd things she has been doing lately. After all, putting that advertisement in the paper was eccentric enough.'

'That was nothing but a bold, if rather foolish, bid for a little belated happiness. Which I may say she deserves.'

'I know she does, but if I told you she was locked in her room at this moment by her own hand,' would you still say she wasn't mad?'

'I would know that whatever Arabia chose to do, she had very sound reasons. She is a wonderful and extraordinary woman. Didn't I tell you that?' Mr. Mullins came as near to glaring as his mild, kindly countenance would permit. Cressida found herself laughing, and her tension lessened. Perhaps it was just another of Arabia's dramatic pranks, in keeping with her secrecy and her love of melodrama.

Nevertheless, when, later in the day, the telephone message came, Mr. Mullins was the first to urge her to hurry home at once. He had taken the message himself. He said, 'Someone is ringing to say that Mimosa is locked in your room, and that you are the only person with a key.'

'Mimosa!' Cressida exclaimed. 'Oh, he must have got shut in this morning after last night. Jeremy and he spent the night—' She blushed suddenly, aware of what she was saying. 'I mean, Jeremy had an extraordinary idea that he should keep an eye on me, after that fall on the stairs, so instead of letting him spend the night on my doorstep I suggested he should sit in the living-room. Mimosa was there, too, and went to sleep on the couch. I remember seeing him there this morning. Oh, how idiotic of me to lock him in.'

'You don't think he could wait now until closing time?' Mr. Mullins suggested.

'Normally, yes, but the other day he was in my room half-poisoned, and last night there was the tin tied to his tail. You don't know, Mr. Mullins! I think there must be a poltergeist or something. And Jeremy so dotes on him.'

Mr. Mullins permitted himself a twinkle.

'Then of course he must be rescued immediately. Run along. And since it's quiet this afternoon there doesn't seem much point in your coming back. Keep an eye on Arabia, or make tea for that doting young man.'

'Mr. Mullins, you are a darling. I adore you,' said Cressida, and flew for her hat and coat.

*   *   *

But when she unlocked the door of her room and went in, there was no sign of Mimosa. She called to him and looked under the couch and the bed. But there was no large, sunflower-coloured cat, no sudden playful spring, no indignant wail. Who had sent that urgent message, she suddenly wondered. Mr. Mullins had omitted to tell her to whom he had spoken. She had assumed it had been Jeremy, but now she wasn't sure, for surely Jeremy would have been awaiting her arrival. There was no one about, and no sound in the house.

She was about to leave the room and go and call Jeremy when she noticed that one door of the big wardrobe in her bedroom was open. Surely she hadn't left it open that morning. And what were all those clothes hanging inside? They were not hers, and neither had they been there before. She had had no more than a suit and a cocktail dress to hang in the wardrobe. They had looked very meagre in the cavernous space, and she had kept the doors firmly shut on the poverty of her wardrobe.

But now there were coloured dresses, a beaver coat, a dark grey suit hanging ostentatiously within. Bewildered, she went over to investigate.

A faint musty scent met her nostrils as she leaned inside the dim space. It was a scent composed of camphor and pot-pourri. Dead roses, she thought, her brain beginning to whirl.

And these dresses were of a style dating back to the nineteen-thirties. Lucy's, she thought in a flash, as she fingered a tarnished silver brocade. And then she had time to think no more, for a strong push from behind sent her suddenly head-long into the wardrobe. She banged her head severely against the farther wall, and darkness came down on her—a musty sweet-smelling darkness shot through faintly with lights as her head throbbed.

The doors had been shut on her.

Now she could not control her panic. Fighting her way upright, among the enveloping clothes, the beaver coat threatening to smother her, she beat on the heavy doors.

'Let me out! Whoever is there! Let me out!'

There was no sound at all. The person who must have been hiding behind the open wardrobe door, anticipating her interest in the unexpected discovery of the clothes, must have pushed her in and slammed the doors in one skilful movement, and now had crept away silently leaving her to suffocate.

No, whoever it was had not gone. Cressida could hear heavy breathing, as of someone leaning against the door listening to her pleas. Listening and laughing, no doubt, with a horrible humourless mirth.

That breathing! It was the sound Arabia had made on the other side of her locked door this morning. The laboured sound of age and deep emotion.

'Arabia!' she sobbed. 'It is you! Let me out, please. This is such an absurd game to play.'

There was a momentary silence, then a deep

hoarse chuckle from without. Cressida beat on the doors. Already she was growing uncomfortably hot, the perspiration starting out on her forehead.

'Arabia! I'll die in here, among Lucy's clothes. You don't mean me to die, do you? You said you loved me.'

There was a faint shuffling sound, then the hoarse whispered voice.

'You should have gone away as I told you to. What right had you to come here stealing Lucy's life? Usurper!'

The dramatic word was spat out. But there was more.

'Stay there and die,' said the malevolent voice.

And then the shuffling sound moved away, farther and farther.

'Arabia!' screamed Cressida in an agony of horror and panic.

There was no answer. The old lady was gone out of hearing. She was alone in the airless darkness, suffocated with the musty odour of a dead girl's clothes.

But there must be someone in the house who would hear her calling and knocking. Miss Glory, Mrs. Stanhope, Jeremy. After his faithful watchdog act last night, surely Jeremy was not far away.

But he thought she was safely at work. He had probably gone out. He would be investigating to see whether Lucy's death were registered under the name of Meredith. Lucy, dearly loved wife of Larry Meredith. Poor Lucy who had no grave, because a crazy old woman would not admit she was dead...

'Jeremy! Mrs. Stanhope! Miss Glory!'

Miss Glory would be out doing the daily shopping, Mrs. Stanhope probably resting in her room that was too far for Cressida's voice to reach it. The inquisitive Dawson who loved murders and foul play would be at work. Oh, Arabia, for all her craziness, had chosen a shrewd time to play this last and most diabolical trick.

It must have been Arabia who had telephoned Mr. Mullins, and he, foolish besotted innocent, had not suspected her story. Neither had Cressida suspected it. The trail had been too well laid. Mimosa had been in danger twice and could so easily have been for a third time.

Was she to die for the sake of a skittish cat who looked like a sunflower?

'Please, please! Someone let me out!'

She was sobbing and growing faint. The stale perfume of roses was overpowering.

This silk brushing her cheek—to what long-ago ball had Lucy worn it, what ghostly echoes of laughter and music did it hold? These furs, how had they muffled Lucy's slender body and framed her little face which looked out like a rose? How could she have wanted to steal Lucy's life, that held so many unhappy secrets—the perhaps unwilling marriage to Larry (yes, that must have been it, Lucy had married him unwillingly), the desperate cry to her lover, 'Darling, darling, darling ...' the pathetically unwanted baby that was destined never to be born.

And now another tragedy was to be added to Lucy's—Cressida's ignominious death in a suffocating darkness, smothered with the dead girl's clothes.

Almost she was growing peaceful about it.

194

Drowsiness was slipping over her. If she died no one would grieve too much. Jeremy, perhaps, for the face he would never now put on to canvas, for the kiss he would never finish. Tom—oh, she had forgotten to read Tom's letter this morning. Poor Tom! She had treated him with as little understanding as he had her. She could not have made him happy, she knew now. Nevertheless, it would distress him deeply to learn that she had died in such an extraordinary way. He would feel that it was another embarrassing slight to his dignity.

He would say, 'Poor little one—' No, it would be Jeremy who would say that. 'What a charming little upsidedown face—surrounded with all that fur and ball dresses—on such a hot day—'

In her growing detachment from her surroundings, Cressida thought she could hear music. But it was not for her. It was for Lucy who was going to a ball. The violins were playing.

From a rumba to a requiem...

The words, coming sharply into her mind, roused her from her growing lethargy. She was not going to die at all! That was Mr. Moretti's violin she could hear. He was in his room down the hall. He must hear her if she called. He must!

In a last desperate effort, Cressida summoned all her energy and shouted and knocked, until her knuckles were grazed and bleeding.

Then she listened. The music had stopped. There were footsteps coming, fingers on the key of the wardrobe. The doors opened.

'Yes—I'm in here—isn't it idiotic!' Cressida whispered, and fell out on to the floor like a puppet dropped from its strings.

CHAPTER SEVENTEEN

Mr. Moretti could not have been kinder. He quickly fetched brandy which he made Cressida drink, then he sat beside her on the couch, talking quietly, helping her to recover.

'Why should she *do* such a horrible thing?' she kept saying. 'She laughed at me. Did she mean me to die in there?'

'Actually I don't think you would have died,' Mr. Moretti said in his calm reassuring way. 'It probably felt terribly stuffy, but a certain amount of air would get in. You panicked, that was the trouble.'

'Wouldn't you have?' Cressida demanded indignantly.

'I certainly would have. In fact, I wouldn't stay in this house another minute if that had happened to me.'

He looked at her with his pale kind eyes. His face was full of concern.

'You think—it's dangerous to stay?'

'I certainly do. You say you have had other warnings. Do you realise each one is getting more serious? You may not have died in the wardrobe, but the next time—'

Cressida began to shiver. In spite of the brandy shock still held her. She was incapable of thinking constructively. Lucy's clothes, sweetly musty, seemed still to be pressing on her, robbing her of animation and breath.

'You must go,' said Mr. Moretti in his serious concerned voice. 'You know now what the position is. Arabia is a Jekyll-and-Hyde person. She may be charming one day, and the next—well, you know for yourself. It's her obsession about Lucy.'

'She really hates me for being alive,' Cressida whispered. 'I didn't think I would ever believe that, but now—'

'Have you enough money to go home?' Mr. Moretti asked. 'If you haven't I'll be glad to lend you some.'

'That's very kind of you, but I have. Mr. Mullins paid me in advance. Oh, dear Mr. Mullins!'

'This is no time to worry about him. Your safety comes first. Isn't that sense? Come now, pack your bag, and I'll take you to the station.'

But Cressida could not move. There was not a great deal to pack in her bag, but she found herself incapable of getting it out and putting things in. It was so short a time since she had happily and excitedly unpacked in this pretty room that Arabia had prepared for her. Just for her, she had thought. But it had really been for Lucy, just as the other pretty room upstairs, forever empty and undisturbed, was for Lucy. Arabia did not want girls who were attractive and young to be alive, she wanted them cold and dead.

'Don't think about it,' came Mr. Moretti's soft persuasive voice. 'Just get away. When you're safely home you'll forget all about it. I'll call Mrs. Stanhope to come and pack for you. She'll understand.'

Before Cressida could stop him he had gone. Presently he came back, on his quick light feet that so easily fitted themselves to a dance, followed by Mrs. Stanhope.

Mrs. Stanhope was out of breath, her eyes enormously distended behind the large glasses. She was like an owl who had been awoken in daylight, full of startled terror.

'You poor child!' she whispered. 'Mr. Moretti told me.'

'He says I must go,' Cressida said helplessly.

'He's right, I'm afraid. Dawson and I have thought so from the beginning. We always knew she'—she pointed eloquently to the ceiling—'had very peculiar motives. Very peculiar. We've heard her talking at night.'

'Talking?'

'To herself. Or to that horrid parrot.' Mrs. Stanhope's hand went to her throat in its familiar protective gesture. She had spoken more than she had ever done in Cressida's presence.

'Dawson will be home shortly,' she whispered. 'He will take you to the station.'

'I'll find out the time of a train for you,' Mr. Moretti said kindly. 'Come along now, you must pull yourself together. You're not actually hurt, you know.'

'Not yet,' Mrs. Stanhope whispered. 'Where is your bag, dear?'

Their concerted energy roused Cressida from her curious state of helplessness and despair. She forced herself to go to the wardrobe and get her bag from the top shelf, then indicate to ·Mrs. Stanhope the clothes that were hers.

Mrs. Stanhope's eyes, at the sight of the limp and old-fashioned garments hanging within, grew even larger. But she said nothing but 'Tch tch' this time, and began briskly to pack the things that Cressida had so energetically and excitedly packed herself a week ago when she had left the house in Oakshott on her adventure into independence and maturity.

She still could not think of anything but the horror of that long, dark, suffocating period in the wardrobe, and obeyed Mrs. Stanhope and Mr. Moretti, who were so anxiously helping her, like an automaton.

'I think she ought to go up and call out goodbye to the old woman,' Mr. Moretti said. 'Don't you think so, Mrs. Stanhope?'

And what about the others: Miss Glory who had always been kind to her, and Jeremy—Jeremy whose impudence had never borne any malice...

'There's no one else in,' Mr. Moretti said, as if he read her thoughts. 'I met Winter down the road catching a bus some time ago, and my rosebud is out shopping.' (Did Mrs. Stanhope flash him a glance of contempt for his facetious reference to Miss Glory?) 'We will have to say your farewells for you. But I think you owe it to yourself to have a little revenge on the old woman. Tell her you're going and are depriving her of her favourite recreation.'

Arabia had confessed that she craved to be amused and diverted. Had her malevolent tricks been for the sake of amusement? It could easily be so.

Cressida, still dazed both from shock and the effects of the large brandy Mr. Moretti had given her, allowed herself to be taken upstairs by Mrs. Stanhope, who solicitously held her arm.

'Is her door still locked?' she asked Mrs.

Stanhope.

Mrs. Stanhope nodded. 'Except when she creeps about the house,' she said in her hoarse whisper.

'I wonder you're not afraid to stay here, too,' Cressida commented.

'We can't afford to do anything else, Dawson and I. And after all it isn't us who have her spite.'

Spite, hatred, resentment—what horrible words they were. Cressida, still in the hold of the nightmare, knocked on the white door and called, 'Arabia! I've come to say goodbye. I'm leaving you.'

'Louder,' urged Mrs. Stanhope.

But it seemed as if Arabia had been lurking inside, listening, for her voice came almost at once.

'What? Who is that? Who is leaving?' as if she were totally unaware of all that had been going on.

The sound of the warm, familiar voice was too much for Cressida. Oh, Arabia, you absurd old woman, I could have loved you! You were so wonderful! she cried silently, and turned and fled downstairs, thinking only now of the train waiting, and the gloomy station, and the telegram she must send to Tom.

The dream—it had all been a dream, fascinating, fearful, delightful—was over.

Dawson came in the front door as she reached the bottom of the stairs. He was suddenly there like a genie, thin and willowy, wreathing out of a bottle.

'Ah, just in time,' said Mr. Moretti with satisfaction. 'You'll see Miss Barclay to her train, won't you?'

Dawson's eyes went from the closed bag to Cressida, dressed for travelling. His glance swiftly met his mother's.

'There's been another—*episode!*' his mother whispered meaningly.

'Coo!' said Dawson. Then he added briskly, 'Sure, I'll take her to the train. I'll get a taxi. That's the safest way. The fog's thick again, funny things happen in fogs. Although it said in the paper today they'd got the murderer of the girl in the red shoes. So all this isn't anything to do with him.'

The nightmare came down on her again. Suddenly she longed above everything to go in the taxi alone. It was bad enough going like this, but to have Dawson beside her gloating over the details of old murders was too much. There was no use, however, in protesting. Someone must go with her, Mr. Moretti said, and if it were not Dawson it would be himself. Perhaps she would prefer him, he suggested, his wide smile spreading over his colourless face.

But for all his kindness, she had even less desire for his company than for Dawson's. If only Jeremy would come out of the fog, striding up the slippery marble steps, mocking her for her lack of courage.

The taxi which Dawson had energetically signalled drew up. Mrs. Stanhope gave her hand a timid squeeze, whispered, 'Cheer up! It's all over now,' and Mr. Moretti, opening the door of the taxi, bowed with his exaggerated courtesy.

'Please understand, Miss Barclay, we're most unselfishly doing this for your safety. Your departure is our loss.'

'Nuts!' muttered Dawson under his breath. 'Say that to Miss Glory.'

Mrs. Stanhope was suddenly backing away up the stairs and gesturing excitedly towards the upstairs window. Cressida looked up and saw the dim shape of Arabia's face pressed against the glass. Her hair was wild, her whole attitude curiously forlorn. Her hands, spread against the glass in a starfish pattern, were helpless and childlike.

The tears sprang into Cressida's eyes. Oh, should she go after all? Poor old lady, alone and in the grip of her unhappy madness. What was going to happen to her?

But Dawson was pushing her into the taxi, and climbing in after her.

'Paddington,' he said briskly to the driver, 'and don't waste time. We have to catch a train.'

The last thing Cressida saw was Mr. Moretti putting his arm round Mrs. Stanhope's waist in a friendly and comforting gesture. With his suave manners and soft words he knew how to be nice to women. Was little Mrs. Stanhope, colourless and self-effacing, blushing in shy embarrassment at his attention?

Dawson had noticed the gesture, too, for his thin body was rigid with distaste.

'Always getting round women,' he said. 'Even Ma doesn't see through him.'

'What is there to see?' Cressida asked.

Dawson wriggled angrily.

'Only that everything he does is for himself, really, even though he pretends it is for other people.'

202

'Even helping me to get away?' Cressida suggested.

'That was sense,' Dawson admitted grudgingly. 'But anyone would have done the same.' Then he forgot his disapproval, and turned eagerly to Cressida. 'Gosh, did the old lady lock you in the wardrobe? Gosh, that was really something. The next thing would have been poison, sure as fate.'

★   ★   ★

The fog swallowed up Dragon House. For Arabia, watching from her upstairs window, it swallowed up the taxi, too, and now she was alone. Truly alone, with no one at all to love her or to divert her from the coming winter. Ever again.

But soon she would know nothing of either spring or winter, because of the danger that lurked. Soon it would take form. The voice that hissed 'I hate you!' would do so for the last time within her mortal hearing.

At first she had been very much afraid, and had locked herself in, listening to every footstep, every sound. But when Cressida had called goodbye through the door, leaving her in spite of all her assurances, the late and so lovely spring had died. All her tender, growing happiness had been extinguished. So now she did not care very much whether her door were locked or not.

With quick pulls of her bony old fingers she completed unravelling a piece of blue wool, knitted into the shape of a tiny sock, and flung it over Ahmed.

'Who would have thought she would have been so easily frightened?' she demanded of the ruffled

203

bird. Ahmed struggled with the clinging wool, and squawked angrily.

'If she is like that it is better for her to go,' Arabia said.

Then she went and unlocked her door, with a loud ostentatious turning of the key, and going back to her brightly-lit untidy room she sat down to wait for the expected footsteps.

CHAPTER EIGHTEEN

Cressida endured Dawson's company as far as Paddington. Then she said peremptorily, 'Go home now. I don't want you to come on the platform with me.'

'But Ma said—'

'Never mind what your mother said. I'm quite capable of getting on a train by myself. Go, now. I want to be alone.'

Dawson shrugged his shoulders huffily, then extended a limp graceless hand. Cressida realised that his sulkiness was very schoolboyish, and was suddenly remorseful.

'I'm sorry, it's just that I can't stand any more talk of murders.'

Dawson nodded solemnly. 'It's because you've been so near it. Coo!'

Then he waved her an awkward but friendly enough farewell, and she was alone.

She bought a ticket and walked on to the platform. The fog swirled over the tracks, and hung in a yellow gloom round the electric lights. There was the usual clatter and smell of smoke and cold polluted air. A train came in and people spilled out and trailed towards the barrier. Cressida could visualise herself at the end of her journey, getting out of the compartment into the cold air, going slowly towards the barrier, looking for Tom's fair head and earnest face.

Suddenly she remembered that she hadn't telephoned Tom to say she was coming home. She just had time to do so. There was a call-box on the other side of the barrier. She picked up her bag and hurried towards it, explaining to the guard her purpose.

The box was empty. She pushed open the door. The interior smelt of stale smoke. It was almost as musty as the wardrobe filled with Lucy's clothes had been. Lucy—the fascination of her half-known story—the warmth of Arabia's affection, so strangely turned to hate—the gentle firm voice of Mr. Mullins insisting that Arabia was wise and sane—the perfume of red roses, the roses that Jeremy—Jeremy! She had a dinner date with him. She had forgotten it. She had not even left a message. Oh, she could not behave in such a rude and thoughtless way. She must go back and make her apologies. She must—but of course she must go back to Dragon House. There was Arabia's face pressed wistfully, like a child's, against the window-pane watching her departure. There were Jeremy and Mimosa in their warm bright basement, surrounded with sketches and colour and inconsequential chatter about a fabulous trip to Paris. There was the ghost of Lucy, like a perfume, like a half-forgotten song...

How could she have panicked and run away? What a poor coward she was. Was her story to have been only half-finished, as was Lucy's? No, this she would see through to the end.

*   *   *

Her newly-found courage remained with her. She paid the taxi driver and went blithely up the steps to the front door. The door was unlocked, the hall brightly lit, but there was no sign of anybody. As if of their own volition her feet carried her past her door to the stairs and straight up them. At Arabia's door she knocked briskly and waited.

Presently there was a slow cautious footstep within (what had happened to make Arabia so strangely suspicious and cautious?).

'Who is it?' came the whispered voice.

'It's me, Cressida. I've come back. Please let me in.'

The door opened slowly. Arabia's face, harrowed and sunken and very old, looked out. The incredulity in it changed to joy.

'My dear child! My dear, dear child!'

Then the dry old hands seized on Cressida's and drew her in. Only when the door was shut and safely locked did the old lady break down, clinging to Cressida, her face ugly and ravaged.

'Hush, darling, hush,' Cressida soothed, as if to a child. 'I'm back now. I didn't mean to go away. I wasn't thinking straight.'

'You shouldn't have come back,' Arabia said harshly. 'You are very foolish. It's much too dangerous.'

Cressida patted her gently.

'I cared enough about you to come back. That's all that really matters, isn't it?'

Arabia's heavily lidded eyes opened wide. Their tenseness left them and they became soft and tender and beautiful. All the magic of her personality was back in her face, giving it the unforgettable quality that so fascinated Cressida.

'Oh, my dear! That's all that ever mattered.'

Nothing was said about the wardrobe incident. Later, when Arabia was less emotional, Cressida would begin to talk of it. Everything, now, had to be brought into the open. But in a little while, when Arabia had regained her self-assured breeziness and was not so obviously a frail and frightened old woman. It was enough, at present, to soothe her, as one would soothe Ahmed's ruffled feathers.

When Miss Glory came in with a tray of tea Arabia had recovered sufficiently to have made an attempt at tidying her room, briskly plumping cushions, straightening chairs, and winding up a length of unravelled pale-blue wool that seemed to be twined over everything. Ahmed, on his perch, furiously preened his feathers and made a few guttural remarks to himself. What a pity he could not talk, Cressida thought. Perhaps he alone, in all the house, knew the truth.

'You back?' said Miss Glory to Cressida. 'Are you mad, or just foolhardy?'

Her flat voice betrayed no surprise. Her sallow face seemed to have taken on a yellow tinge, and her eyes were lifeless. Was she ill, Cressida wondered. Or just suddenly desperately unhappy.

But what had happened to change her from her almost juvenile coyness to this look of having plumbed the depths of disillusion? Obviously it was something Mr. Moretti had done, and equally obviously he was unaware of his fall from grace.

Without waiting for Cressida to give an explanation about her return, she went on:

'Our artist friend will be delighted. He went haring off to Paddington like a wild thing when he heard you had gone. If you ask me, his interest in you is more than academic. More fool he! Love! What is it but a snare and a delusion?' Her lifeless gaze went to Arabia. 'You've got Miss Barclay to do your tasting for you tonight, so I'll go.

Arabia started up. 'No. You must do it as usual. I cannot let Cressida risk her life.'

'Ho!' said Miss Glory in her contemptuous voice. 'And what has she been doing all this week? Very well, I'll risk my entirely worthless life once more. She has this crazy idea,' she explained to Cressida, 'that the food might be poisoned.'

Cressida's heart sank. That was so typical a form of delusion that it alone seemed proof that Arabia was not in full possession of her senses. Indeed, when she saw Arabia's tense interest in Miss Glory's delicate tasting of the tea, the nicely browned omelet, the thin bread and butter, she could only have her fears that the old lady's mind was affected confirmed.

Miss Glory sat back and said, 'Well! I'm still alive and feeling fine.'

Arabia gave her warm transfiguring smile.

'Thank you, Miss Glory. That is very good and courageous of you. Now bring me another cup and saucer for Cressida. Then we'll all feel a great deal better. By the way, Cressida, I had my solicitor here today. I have given him instructions about my new will, and tomorrow he will bring it for my signature.'

'Arabia—'

'Not a word, dear child. I admit it shook me when you said that you were leaving, but even then I did not intend to change my instructions. Now, not a word. Let me pour you some tea. Then we'll be gay. Oh, how nice it will be to be gay again.'

When she had drunk her tea Cressida said that she must go down to see Jeremy and make her excuses about dinner that evening. Arabia clutched at her. Fear was back, nakedly, in her face.

'Don't be long, dear. Don't leave me alone. I have no courage left. I'm a cowardly old woman.'

Cressida promised to return at once, and hurried downstairs. She thought that once again she was going to be fortunate and escape being seen, but the sharp-eared Dawson could not be evaded. He emerged on to the landing and exclaimed.

'Coo! Miss Barclay! Whatever made you come back?'

'I forgot something,' Cressida replied, as airily as possible.

'Coo! Right into the hornet's nest! My, Ma will be upset. Now she will stay awake all night again, listening.'

Cressida knew that she ought to be grateful to the Stanhopes for their interest in her welfare. But suddenly their curiosity and their little apprehensive gloating minds were unendurable.

'There's no need for her to do that,' she said coolly. 'I'm quite able to look after myself.'

She wasn't, of course. If it had not been for Mr. Moretti she would have at least fainted, if not died, in the wardrobe. But the thought of Dawson, with his unhealthy love of violence, and his inquisitive, eternally whispering mother revolted her and made her want to escape their vigilance.

'I think you're crazy!' Dawson's voice followed her down the stairs. But now she was listening no longer, for at the bottom of the basement stairs Jeremy's door stood open and a welcoming shaft of light shone out.

She went quietly and in a self-contained way into the room and said, 'I'm sorry I'm late, but I did come.'

He was standing in the middle of the room. He had on a raincoat and his hair was damp with mist. Mimosa was on the table, arching his back and calling for attention. But Jeremy had been too preoccupied to see him.

It was only Cressida's entry and her apologetic voice that aroused him. His head shot up, the grimness began to leave his face, his dark eyes began to shine.

'Don't do that again! Don't *do* it again!' he said, and strode towards her and took her in his arms.

CHAPTER NINETEEN

But again his kiss, which was too warm and disturbing—so disturbing that she preferred not to think about it—was brief. She firmly loosened herself from his grip and said.

'Jeremy! This isn't the time for that sort of thing. Too many things are happening.'

210

'Do you underestimate the importance of this particular happening?'

Cressida would not meet his bright, tender eyes.

'It isn't a happening—well, one of any stature, at least. We've got to think of other things.'

'Why you almost ran away—'

'And where you were when I got that telephone call about Mimosa, which was obviously a trick.'

'Who did that?'

'I don't know. Mr. Mullins took it. He didn't think to ask questions, of course. And I thought it would be you.'

'I,' said Jeremy, 'was out making a routine check. I've verified one more thing, that if Lucy Bolton didn't die, Lucy Meredith didn't die either.'

'She married someone else after Larry's death,' Cressida said swiftly. 'Perhaps Monty. Perhaps the man to whom she began that letter. She had another name. She must have.'

'That well may be,' said Jeremy. 'But it is no more the immediate thing than that other thing that we will postpone until later this evening.'

'That kiss—' began Cressida and blushed.

'The immediate thing,' said Jeremy imperturbably, 'is that I want you to invite Arabia down to your room for the night.'

'To my room?' Cressida repeated uncertainly. 'But—'

'Yes, I know you've had a horrible fright this afternoon. But believe me, this is important.'

'Jeremy—you think she may really be in danger? That she isn't imagining it at all?'

Jeremy took her hands. 'Why did you come

back after you had run away?' he asked simply.

'Because—because I kept thinking how kind and sweet Arabia is, and how grieved she would be that I had gone. I saw her looking out of the window; she looked stricken, as if the last thing had gone out of her life. I know she is seeing Lucy in me, and there is this horrid thing about her money, too, but I—I had to come back.'

'And that's why you'll have Arabia in your room tonight, from love, and not from fear.'

'But supposing she won't stay?'

'I've thought of that. You'll make her some hot chocolate, and put this in it.

He held out her palm and dropped a small white tablet into it. Her startled eyes met his.

'It's quite harmless,' he said lightly. 'It will only make her sleep, and I should think she could do with a good night's rest. Now just one other thing is important.'

'Yes?'

'It would be better if you could get her down without anyone seeing you.'

'But that's impossible. You know what the Stanhopes are. And Miss Glory prowls. And Mr. Moretti doesn't miss much either, though thank goodness for that this afternoon.'

'Moretti leaves for his night-club at ten o'clock. I'll undertake to keep the rest of them occupied. At five minutes past ten bring Arabia down. Say you want her to have supper with you. Anything. And now, I think it might be wise for you to go up to her again. At five minutes past ten, remember.'

This afternoon she had heard Arabia's hoarse vindictive voice hoping that she died shut in the

212

wardrobe, smothering among Lucy's clothes. Now she was to have the same old lady as her guest, to be welcomed and protected.

Cressida looked at Jeremy's suddenly bleak and earnest face. She looked at the small mysterious tablet in her hand. She was full of cold apprehension, but the same compulsion that she had felt at the railway station was on her. She knew that she was going to do as Jeremy bade her, without further question or indeed understanding.

It was not surprising that Mrs. Stanhope was lying in wait for her, a fearful figure with hands wrung into a bleached whiteness, as she went up the stairs again. Naturally Dawson had gone hotfoot to his mother with the news of her return.

'Miss Barclay! Whatever made you come back?' The question was asked in an agonized whisper.

'I wanted to,' she said calmly. 'I like to finish things.'

'Finish things!' Mrs. Stanhope gave a voiceless laugh that would have been hysterical had it been audible. 'But that's exactly what will happen. To you!' Her bony white finger pointed tremblingly at Cressida.

'I don't think so,' said Cressida, still speaking calmly, although the drama of the trembling little figure was bringing back her own feeling of something cold and sinister constantly lurking in this house. 'I just remember that Arabia was kind and sweet to me, and I owe her this, in spite of everything.'

Mrs. Stanhope produced her pad and wrote with a hand that shook uncontrollably, 'You think she might make it worth your while, but it won't be if you lose your life.'

Cressida angrily pushed the pad back at her.

'That's an intolerable thing to say. I'm sorry, Mrs. Stanhope, but if you believe that, I can only despise you.'

'Nobody really despises money,' came Dawson's voice from the doorway.

'I know how crazy she is,' Mrs. Stanhope wrote emphatically. 'Being up here, I hear things.' She turned to appeal to her son. 'She does it at her own risk, doesn't she?' she whispered helplessly.

Dawson shrugged his shoulders.

'If she shuts her eyes to things, we can't open them. We helped her to go and she's come back, so it can't be our worry any more.'

'It never was your worry,' Cressida said coldly, and went along the passage to Arabia's door.

But as she reached there she turned involuntarily and saw the pair watching her, as if hypnotised. Mrs. Stanhope's hands were being wrung again, and even Dawson, for all his laconic indifference, had the shine of perspiration on his brow. His eyes looked enormous.

They really had got the jitters, Cressida thought, trying to dismiss lightly their terrified attitude. Living up here, so close to Arabia, they probably did know more than other people; heard things, perhaps, in the night. And one had to agree that they had combined loyalty to Arabia (or was it merely the fear of losing the roof over their heads?) with thought for Cressida's safety, when one recalled their energetic assistance in her leave-taking that afternoon.

Everyone in the house tried to protect her from whatever form Arabia's craziness might take—except Jeremy who now encouraged her to

214

be at the old lady's side, rubbing shoulders with danger, so to speak.

But when one saw Arabia it was all so absurd and unbelievable. For now, her spirits revived at Cressida's return, she had changed into one of her long picturesque gowns, and put on her jewels and her tiara, which, at this moment, was miraculously straight. She greeted Cressida in a queenly manner.

'Come in, my dear. Is Jeremy very cross with me for stealing you? Ah, but he isn't in danger of his life this night.' She led Cressida into her brilliantly lighted room, where every lamp glowed, and Ahmed sat ruffled sulkily on his perch, his eyes resolutely shut.

'I adore soft lights,' Arabia went on. 'But not tonight. Tonight we must be alert, we must watch every shadow, listen to every sound.

In her own way she was being as melodramatic as Mrs. Stanhope, but here was no trembling cowardice, rather an almost pleasurable anticipation of danger. Arabia's head was very erect, her eyes gleaming, her manner full of defiance. In the hour since Cressida's return she had recaptured her inimitable vitality. She seemed to have shaken herself out of her fear and was ready to face and defy her mysterious enemy.

'Arabia, why do you think you are in danger?' Cressida asked.

'I don't think it, my child. I know it. Doesn't the whole house breath it?' She waved her ringed hands and her tiara slipped sideways. 'Vultures! Vultures, all of them!' At the apparently familiar word Ahmed jerked his head out of his feathers, muttered bad-temperedly, and settled himself to

215

sleep again.

Then Arabia gave her brilliant smile and patted Cressida's hand soothingly. 'After tomorrow it will be all right. Just keep your courage until then. Oh, I have faced worse situations than this. There was the time in Tibet when my husband and I were taken prisoner by a hostile tribe of Mongols. Have you ever lived on sour goat's milk? No, of course you haven't. Death, in comparison, is a trifling affair. And even with the sheik there were moments when death was preferable to dishonour.' This last cryptic statement Arabia did not go on to elucidate. She straightened her tiara with a quick tilt, and went on talking, the dam of her two days' silence and solitary imprisonment broken, and life, even in retrospect, became irresistibly glamorous.

Cressida kept her eyes on the clock. At one stage she heard the thin wailing of Mr. Moretti's violin—he was playing his favourite elegy once more—and several times she heard quick footsteps, Dawson's, she surmised, on the stairs.

At ten o'clock she stopped the flow of Arabia's reminiscences and said, 'It's time you got some rest, you know. What about me making you some hot chocolate?'

'That would be delightful, my dear. How thoughtful of you.'

'But I want you to come down and have it in my room. After all, you've never really visited me there.'

'In your room?' Arabia's eyelids fell, covering her thoughts.

'It will be a little change for you,' Cressida continued brightly. 'You haven't been out of these

216

rooms for twenty-four hours. Now—if you don't come I'll think you're suspicious of me, too.'

Arabia started up.

'Not of you, dear child. No, no, I couldn't bear that, too. Very well, we will go to your room and drink hot chocolate. Yes, it will be a change for me.' She was vigorously shaking off her secret fear. 'Just look, will you, my dear, and see that there is no one about. I dislike everybody in the house knowing my movements. Ahmed, beautiful one, you must stay here and keep watch. There, you will be quite safe, my pretty.'

The Stanhopes' door, Cressida discovered, was safely shut. The door of the ballroom was also shut and through it came the distant murmur of voices. Cressida could identify Jeremy's, but no other one.

She reported that the coast was clear, and found Arabia at her side, suddenly all eagerness and excitement.

'My dear, such a clever idea!' the old lady was whispering. 'They won't think to look for me there. Come, quickly now! Not a sound.'

It was all a gigantic joke. The wardrobe in the bedroom was shut, safely concealing the pathetic, mustily-sweet dresses that once had been worn so gaily and confidently by the dead Lucy. Arabia sat on the red velvet couch, a tipsy-looking queen now, with her tiara once more tilted over one ear, and laughed with the glee of a child.

'Outwitted!' she said in her hoarse whisper. 'Such a brilliant idea.'

Was it true, then, that everything she did was a game? Her exultation in this one seemed to suggest that that was true. The locked doors, the

torn-up notes, the roses with their sinister card ...
Sometimes, of course, mere games would grow
anæmic and boring, so occasionally they were
invested with danger. The mock-poisonings, the
suffocating wardrobe...

In the tiny kitchen, out of sight of Arabia,
Cressida dissolved the white tablet in the hot
milk. Then she mixed the chocolate and brought
it in. The old lady took the cup and sipped with
enjoyment.

'You didn't want that tasted to see if it were
poison?' Cressida commented.

'My dear child, no!'

'Then why is poor Miss Glory so suspect?'

'The woman's a fool.' Arabia drank again,
sinking deeper into the comfortable couch, her
tiara resting crazily on her left ear. 'Vultures!' she
ejaculated startlingly in her deep tones.

Cressida sat at her feet, adoring her
picturesqueness, her unexpectedness.

The old lady's heavily ringed hand rested a
moment on her head.

'Once Lucy used to do that,' she said, and it
was the first time she had voluntarily mentioned
Lucy's name for two days.

'Arabia! Lucy did marry Larry, didn't she?'

The hand slid away. 'Yes, she married him.'

'Didn't you approve of him?'

'Approve of him? Oh, yes. He was a nice lad.
Not equal to Lucy, perhaps. I was afraid of that.
But I gave her a beautiful wedding.'

'Yes,' said Cressida softly. 'I saw the
photograph.'

'The photograph?' Arabia stirred. 'You found
out too much, minx.'

218

'Mr. Mullins had it. He thought I should find it, but I don't know why.'

'Albert Mullins!' Arabia's voice was just slightly blurred. 'A loyal friend, indeed. But he pried, too. Everybody pried.'

'Why shouldn't they have? Arabia, if Lucy were married to Larry, why did it matter about the baby?'

'What baby?'

Cressida looked up into Arabia's shrouded eyes. She took the empty cup and put it safely down.

'But of course you know about the baby. You told me. That was why Lucy died, you said.'

'Did I say that?' Arabia's voice was vaguely astonished. 'My dear, I tell so many stories. All those about the sheik—not strictly true, you know. My husband would not have permitted—'

'The baby, Arabia. Lucy's baby. We're talking about that.'

'I had a piece of blue wool,' Arabia said dreamily. 'I unravelled it. All of it. It was no shape any more. It's finished. Over. You gave it to me,' she said accusingly.

Cressida leaned forward. Oh, why had she given Arabia the tablet so soon? The old lady was almost asleep. Who would have thought it would work so quickly. But without it, would Arabia have talked at all?

'Arabia! Open your eyes! Tell me why Larry died. Please! It's important.'

'Larry!' the old lady said thickly. Suddenly she lifted her arm in an attempt to shield her eyes, as if she were deeply, desperately afraid. The next instant it was too heavy for her to hold. It slipped to her side, her head dropped and she was asleep.

Cressida gently removed the tiara from the carefully dressed grey hair. Then she eased the sleeping figure into a recumbent position. Arabia looked very grand lying there, in her rich dress, the jewels sparkling around her neck and blooming on her knotty fingers. Her ugliness was noble, majestic. With all her love of drama, she had never created more than now, as she lay sleeping in her carefully preserved grandeur on Cressida's couch, while outside, perhaps upstairs, perhaps in the marble-floored hall, the danger she feared so much lurked.

The fog had turned to rain. Cressida could hear it whispering against the window, and a wind, too, rattled the frames intermittently. The streets were quiet, only an occasional footstep or a fast-moving car passing.

The house, too, was quiet. What was everybody doing? Mrs. Stanhope and Dawson would have gone to their virtuous beds, but even in sleep their ears would be standing out attentively. Miss Glory, poor Miss Glory with her obscure disillusion in her face, might be pottering in the kitchen, but more likely she, too, would be lying in her narrow bed in the corner of the ballroom beneath the elaborately carved ceiling. Mr. Moretti, safely out of the house, would have forsaken his elegies and be playing light-hearted dance music, Jeremy—he was the mystery. He was up to something. But now Cressida's trust in him was complete. She knew that she would obey him, no matter what extraordinary thing he told her to do.

She carefully shut all the doors into this room, prudently turning the key in the one leading into the hall. Then, wakeful but relaxed, she sat down to wait. She was not afraid. Arabia, she thought, had been the prankster, the malicious practical joker, and Arabia was safely here, sound asleep and harmless. So what had she of which to be afraid?

Hush! Was that someone walking overhead in Arabia's rooms? Cressida listened intently. She thought she could hear furtive footsteps. Was there someone prowling through Arabia's rooms, expecting to find a defenceless old woman there? No all was silent again. There hadn't been anyone. She had imagined it. It was only the intermittent bump of the window frame in the wind, the gusty sound of rain.

Arabia breathed heavily and rhythmically. Cressida turned out all the lights except the one over the fireplace. The shadowed room made her drowsy. It had been a long, exciting day. She was more tired than she had realised. It was safe to sleep. Quite safe. Jeremy was up to something, but he knew what he was doing. There was nothing to worry about.

And then Ahmed gave a small disturbed squawk! It was little more than a hoarse grunt, but the sound was horrifying in the silent house. Cressida watched to see if Arabia would stir, roused by her pet's familiar voice. But she made no movement, and now there was silence upstairs, too, as if Ahmed had not been frightened, but merely grumbled in his sleep.

Nevertheless, Cressida kept visualising the dark room, its brilliant colours extinguished, and imagining a prowler bumping into a standard lamp, stumbling over a cushion on the floor, inadvertently clinging to Ahmed's perch. Someone who did not mean to put on a light, who preferred to be in the dark...

Perhaps Arabia's intuition of danger was not imaginary after all. Cressida moved a little nearer to the unconscious figure, protectively. Now the silence lasted a long time. Cressida had been in a half sleep, aware vaguely of the rain, and the hoarse breathing beside her, but of nothing else, when she started up, hearing the front door open and click shut. There were brisk footsteps across the hall. Another door opened.

That was Mr. Moretti home from his night-club. Surely he was home early tonight. Yes, it was scarcely midnight. Usually it was three or even four o'clock before he came in. Did that mean anything significant?

But there had been nothing furtive about his return. He had come in in his usual manner, and almost instantly his arrival was followed by Mimosa giving his plaintive high-pitched miaow in the hall.

That, thought Cressida, her heart beating rapidly, meant that Jeremy's door was open, and Jeremy—what was he doing?

Nothing, apparently, for the minutes went on and the house remained silent once more.

Cressida's sudden overpowering tiredness made her impatient and irritable. If something were to happen, why didn't it happen? In a moment she would go out and find Jeremy, and demand to know—

Oh! There was the furtive footsteps upstairs again. This time Ahmed did squawk with loud abandon, and Arabia awoke.

She cried in a dreadful voice, 'Lucy!' and struggled to her feet. There she stood swaying, trying to keep her heavy eyelids open, a look of nightmare horror on her face.

'I must go up,' she said thickly. 'I must face her.' She began to stumble towards the door.

Cressida ran to prevent her. She gripped the old lady's arm.

'No, Arabia! You mustn't go upstairs. Jeremy said you mustn't.'

Arabia, with a magnificent effort of will, was throwing off her drugged sleepiness. She flung up her head and looked at Cressida from hooded haughty eyes.

'And what right has Jeremy to forbid me to go to my own rooms? This is not Jeremy's affair. It is mine and my daughter's. Leave go of me, please. I must face her.'

'Arabia, Lucy isn't upstairs! It's someone else—'

But Ahmed had squawked again, and Arabia had flung off Cressida's detaining hand and made for the door.

'Courage!' she was hissing to herself. 'Courage!'

There was nothing Cressida could do but follow the suddenly strong and purposeful old figure to the stairs.

'Arabia, Lucy isn't up there. She's dead. You've told me yourself.

There was a sudden stifled scream from the direction of Arabia's rooms. Arabia paused. Her eyes went glassy. She gripped the stair post.

'Hurry!' she said, but now it seemed as if she could no longer persuade her legs to move. She looked imploringly at Cressida. 'Lucy is killing somebody. It's meant to be me. She's making a mistake. Tell her, quickly.'

This isn't real, Cressida was thinking numbly. Arabia is having a nightmare caused by that sleeping pill. Lucy isn't upstairs killing anybody. And Jeremy said I was not to leave Arabia.

But who had screamed?

And against her will her feet were carrying her up the stairs.

She had got no farther than half a dozen steps when a voice, high-pitched and feminine, rang shockingly through the house.

'A-aa-h! Yah! Poisoner! Jezebel!'

Then there was a flurry of footsteps, a bump on the floor as of someone springing out of bed, and again the flying footsteps. Suddenly someone screamed. It was not the voice that had spoken first. It was another voice, shrill, long-drawn, in an access of terror. Then there came an awful thudding down the stairs, the beautiful curving marble stairs that were Arabia's pride, as someone tripped and fell.

Cressida, flattened against the banisters, was paralysed. She could not have moved forward to catch that hurtling figure, even had the fall already not done a major injury.

In the split second that followed, everyone seemed to be there, Mr. Moretti, still in dinner jacket, Dawson, half-way down the stairs, a huddled almost childish figure in his pyjamas, Miss Glory in a tightly wrapped dressing-gown, with her grey hair surprisingly done in elaborate curls, and Jeremy beside Arabia, both on their knees bending over the still figure of Mrs. Stanhope.

She was smaller than her son Dawson and even more childlike. Her heavy glasses had fallen off, or she had not been wearing them, and her colourless pointed face was no longer owlish but thin and foxy, the lips drawn back a little, the eyes half open.

As Jeremy put his hand to her breast she gave a little shudder and lay still. He bent closer. Then he raised his head. He looked straight at Mr. Moretti, whose open mouth disclosed the dark cavern of its interior.

'Get a doctor,' he said curtly. 'But I think it's too late to do anything for your wife.'

'Wife!' whispered Miss Glory, her face a piece of parchment.

'M-ma!' stuttered Dawson. His voice was that of a frightened child, ending in an uncontrollable tremor.

But it was Arabia, dishevelled, gaunt, suddenly very old, who had the answer to the riddle. She raised her head with slow impressive dignity and said very quietly:

'Lucy! She's dead at last.'

CHAPTER TWENTY

Lucy! Before anybody could say anything Miss Glory had suddenly bounded up the stairs, and disappeared into Arabia's room. In a moment she reappeared, carrying a glass of water. She came down the stairs slowly, as if she were bearing something very precious. Her eyes, cold and malignant, rested on Mr. Moretti.

225

'This will prove an interesting analysis, no doubt,' she said in her flat expressionless voice. 'I may even give it to you for your morning tea, *Mr. Moretti.*'

Mr. Moretti put out a defensive hand. All the pale pinkness had gone out of his face. It was startlingly white, and in comparison his usually colourless brows and lashes were like yellow honey. His lips worked.

'It was her—not me!' he got out. 'She—knew the tricks. You must—realise that—'

But Dawson, suddenly jerked into life, pointed a long thin forefinger fiercely at Mr. Moretti. His face was drawn with hate.

'But only because of you! Only because of you, you b—'

Jeremy put his hand on the boy's trembling shoulder.

'Steady, old man. Be careful what you say. I imagine you haven't entirely clean hands yourself.'

Dawson jerked his head triumphantly.

'But I have! There's nothing in that water but a bit of harmless powder. You can analyze it as much as you like. You can't prove a thing.'

Mr. Moretti started forward.

'You mean, you little double-crosser, that you didn't do it?'

'Did you think I was going to let Ma get into that sort of trouble again? Oh, it was all right while we were just fooling around, giving people frights. That was good fun. But I never meant to do the real thing. Oh, no! Not for all the blasted money in the world.' He turned and shot Mr. Moretti one more glance of pure hate. 'And not to make you wealthy, you poor scared worm. You haven't any guts, that's what's wrong with you. Made us do it all. I never want to set eyes on you again.'

Then suddenly realisation of what had happened seemed to come to him and he went down on his knees beside the little still figure.

'Oh, Ma!' he sobbed. 'Oh, Ma!'

Mrs. Stanhope (Lucy Bolton, Lucy Meredith, Lucy Montgomery, alias Moretti) lay on the bed in the carefully preserved room upstairs, the room that had waited so long for her to come back. She lay on the pretty silk coverlet, with her possessions about her, her old ball dresses, her half-finished diary, her empty perfume bottle, her jewellery, girlish and inexpensive, the locket set with seed pearls that she had worn to Arabia's party round her neck, and on her broken body the satin wedding-dress which she had worn to her wedding with Larry.

She looked young and innocent now, her hair neatly done, a rose in her folded hands. But there was still a look of secrecy about her mouth, an air of wilfulness to her pointed chin. Death could not take from her, all at once, her greed and slyness, her skills as an actress and her utter ruthlessness.

At first Arabia had wept bitterly. It was she who had asked that Mrs. Stanhope be laid in the room upstairs.

'You understand I am not weeping for this woman whom you knew,' she said, with dignity. 'It is for my little girl, my lost Lucy, whom I loved so much, that I weep.'

She admitted that ever since the night of the party she had known Mrs. Stanhope's true identity. At first Mrs. Stanhope had successfully hidden it behind the big glasses and the whispering voice that was merely a clever act. She had changed a great deal in the fifteen years since Arabia had seen her, her hair was white and she had grown prematurely old. She had also had a type of prettiness that in youth was extremely attractive, but which in middle age was quite nondescript. She had suspected that her voice would have been the most likely thing to arouse memory, so she had most skilfully hidden it and only once had her vigilance been found wanting. That had been the night when Cressida had heard her scream, because Mr. Moretti, impatient about the lack of success of their plan, had threatened her with his hands round her throat.

But on the night of the party, when Arabia had suddenly announced that Cressida was to be her heir, Mrs. Stanhope had decided that it was time to reveal herself. She had gone upstairs, ostensibly to change the dress on which wine had been spilt, but in reality to put on the locket which Arabia had given her for her eighteenth birthday, and which she could not fail to recognise.

Arabia had recognised it, and her enemy, in the same moment. That was when she had begun to lock herself in, knowing that she was in extreme danger until her will was irrevocably signed and witnessed.

'But surely your own daughter would not have harmed you,' Cressida whispered in horror.

'She was not my true daughter,' Arabia replied. 'She was my sister's child. She only lived with me for four years, which perhaps explains why I didn't at once recognise her when she came back.

It was not as if I had known her from birth. My sister had married a man who subsequently turned out to be a scoundrel, a thoroughly bad person. He left her, and later she died, when Lucy was only fifteen. That was when Lucy became my daughter. So sweet and pretty and lovable she was then. Oh, no doubt I spoilt her, but who would not have? I could afford to, and she was all I had. So there were the parties and gaiety I told you about. All of that was true. The roses, and the admirers and the laughter. And Larry, her first husband. He was a nice lad and he adored her. They had a beautiful wedding—a pair of children they looked.'

Arabia paused to wipe her eyes. Almost at once the tenderness left her face, and it became harsh and ugly.

'Larry died three years after their wedding,' she said starkly. 'He was poisoned.'

'Not by Lucy,' Cressida gasped.

'By Lucy. By his sweet and loving wife. Oh, not without incitement, I grant you. Not without the encouragement of her wicked lover, Monty. He got five years as an accessory, but it should have been more—much more.'

'Monty!' Cressida whispered, carried away by Arabia's terrible melodrama.

'Yes, Monty. Or Moretti. Whichever you like. Didn't I say he was a caterpillar, a creeping slug. How could she have loved him so disastrously?'

'His name was in the diary. And there was that half-begun letter. And the baby! She was going to have Monty's baby. That's why she didn't hang.'

All at once Arabia looked unbearably weary.

'Heaven be my witness, I didn't know about the

baby. She came here, you see, after Larry's death and before her arrest. There was actually a period of a few weeks when Larry's death was thought to be from natural causes. An acute case of gastro-enteritis, the doctor said. But the nurse had been suspicious. Anyway, later Lucy was arrested here, in this house. The sorrowful little widow whom I had comforted—ah, I had been so sad—while all the time she sat upstairs writing about Monty in an old diary she picked up.'

'The missing pages,' Cressida said. 'You tore them out.'

'I destroyed all that part of Lucy's life,' Arabia said simply. 'I decided that from the day of her marriage to Larry she no longer existed. In my mind I had her die a tragic and innocent death. I tell you, it was the only way I could remain sane.'

'But—she still lived.'

'Not for me. She was her father's daughter then, not her mother's. She was nothing of me. I cast her out.'

Even then Cressida found the old lady's ruthless grandeur impressive and admirable. It was so typical of her. All her life she had admitted only colour and love and drama and happiness, never sadness and defeat. So this most terrible defeat had to be shut out of her mind, treated as if it had never existed. Only a person with such will-power and imagination and vitality could have done it.

But old age had found her weak spot, her loneliness, her longing for the charm and gaiety Lucy's companionship had once brought her.

'Believe me, I knew nothing of the baby,' she said now. 'Even had I known—what would I have

230

done, I wonder? But I knew nothing until the night you brought me that scrap of a sock. Oh, the shock of that revelation!'

'The baby was Dawson,' Cressida said.

Here Jeremy, who had been listening silently, interposed with a brisk explanation.

'He was born in gaol, after Lucy had begun serving her life sentence. His father, who of course knew of his existence, totally ignored him. He was brought up in an orphanage and had started work as an errand boy in a grocer's shop when his mother came out of gaol. She immediately sought him out and gave him a little of the love he had never before known. The consequence of this was that he began to admire everything the devious little woman planned. She knew that there was no use in coming here and making herself known to Arabia as the prodigal daughter—so she came in disguise, with the simple plan of having Dawson worm his way into his great-aunt's affection. Being a doting mother, which was perhaps understandable after her long term in prison, it didn't occur to her that not everyone might find her son as attractive as she herself did. As for Dawson, being admired and loved went to his head. And there is the fact that he has a good brain. He got this job in a chemist's shop, and began to take an unhealthy interest in drugs and poisons. One never knew when it would come in useful, he said. Moretti turning up was unexpected. There is a vulture if you like.'

Arabia nodded energetically. 'Vulture, yes! No courage of his own to kill, but oh, his greed to get at dead bodies!'

Cressida shivered. Jeremy went on quietly.

'Moretti found he could exercise his old spell over Lucy. He had expected her to come back here for a reconciliation with her wealthy adopted mother, and he did not intend to be done out of any of the pickings. When he saw that no reconciliation had taken place, he decided to move in and help things along.' Jeremy flung out his hands. 'Well—the rest you know.'

'No, I don't,' said Cressida vigorously. 'What about all those things that happened to me, and which—' She turned to Arabia. 'Forgive me, darling—I thought you had done them.'

'It suited them to say I was crazy,' Arabia said. 'Perhaps I am a little. But not in that way. I didn't frighten you, my dear.'

'It was mostly Dawson,' Jeremy said. 'He had an extraordinary facility for moving silently and thinking up nasty tricks. It was he who locked you in Lucy's room and sent you those death notices and followed you in the fog. He gave his mother a harmless mixture to make her sick that night, and he also gave Mimosa a pill that made him dopey for a while. He took a morbid pleasure in spreading stories about poison and murders. In fact, he's a thoroughly twisted character, poor boy.'

'The wardrobe?' Cressida asked.

'That was Moretti. Staged and executed by the maestro himself, who, incidentally, is an excellent mimic. He left you there just long enough to get thoroughly panicky and then he hastened your departure from the house. Actually, if you hadn't come back that night Arabia would not have been in danger, because they would have reverted to their original plan of inveigling Dawson into her affections. But when you came back they saw that she had to die before the will making you her heir was executed. After all, even if Dawson hadn't succeeded in obtaining her passionate affection—and there was no will—Lucy would have inherited as next of kin. But a will leaving everything to you would be fatal. So when you came back action had to be taken.'

'How did you know all this?' Cressida asked, with respect. 'How did you know that Arabia must not be in her room that night?'

'Because that day I was in bed with 'flu,' Jeremy told her, 'no one in the house knew I was there, and I overheard one illuminating word.'

'What was that?'

'A voice I didn't recognise—but which of course I know now was Mrs. Stanhope's—saying "Monty". So I knew the enemy was right here. But at that stage I was afraid he would strike at you.'

'So you sat up all night,' Cressida murmured.

'That,' said Jeremy, 'was no hardship.'

'Get on with the story,' said Arabia imperiously. 'Keep your love-making until later.'

Cressida's eyes met Jeremy's and dropped in startled acknowledgement. With an effort she concentrated on the rest of his story.

'This is where Miss Glory comes into it. As you know, she had been in an extraordinarily besotted state about Moretti, who apparently couldn't resist exercising his charm over any woman, no matter what her age or appearance. But she was completely disillusioned on the night of the party. When Mimosa ran down the stairs (with the tin the charming Dawson had tied to his tail), and

Cressida, following him, slipped, Miss Glory knew the truth. It was no accidental fall. Cressida had been pushed. And by Moretti. Miss Glory saw him do it. Naturally she was shattered. She planned revenge. Finally, she confided in me and we worked out a plan. We suspected an attempt would be made on Arabia's life last night, before she had had an opportunity to complete her will, so we had her go down to you, Cressida, and Miss Glory got into her bed. She did it very creditably, too, with her hair curled, and Ahmed on the bedpost. Ahmed knew the difference, though, and kept squawking, as you heard. He startled Lucy and made her give a small scream.'

'Lucy?'

'Everyone knew that Arabia, on waking, drank the glass of water that was placed at her bedside the night before. Mrs. Stanhope had thought it would be so simple to switch tumblers, the one she substituted containing the colourless but lethal dose of poison which Dawson had provided. Miss Glory lay still long enough for the tumblers to be changed. Then you heard the rest.'

Cressida, indeed, remembered the wild accusing cry that had come from upstairs, and then the shriek, that awful terrified shriek...

'We didn't mean the woman to die,' Jeremy said.

Arabia moved at last.

'It's better,' she said. 'It's much better. What was there for her?' Her face contorted. 'Poor scrap,' she whispered, and now her difficult tears were not for the girl Lucy but for little Mrs. Stanhope, mousy, nervous, the ex-convict who had fallen once more into scheming and error.

'I must do something for the boy,' she said. 'He showed decency, and courage, too, at the end. A good school, a profession. What do you say, Cressida?'

Cressida replied eagerly, 'Yes, you must do that. And really, Arabia, I don't want your money. I never did. I only let you think so because I didn't want to hurt your feelings.'

'Bless you!' said the old lady. 'Bless you, child. Let me tell you a secret. Most of my jewels are false. And this house is mortgaged. It was the influence of the sheik, really. He encouraged me to be extravagant. I played ducks and drakes with my fortune. But, oh, I had a fine time. A most exciting and glamorous time. Life was never dull then. Why,' she said, her eyes opening to their brilliant warmth, 'life isn't dull now. Oh, but yes, I see it is. You two want to be alone. Very well, be alone. I'll leave you. After all, I have Ahmed and Miss Glory. And the boy. Yes, the boy. I must do something for him ...'

She went out, her tall body erect, her face suddenly full of eagerness and interest. She was a wonderful, a remarkable old woman, but at the moment neither Cressida nor Jeremy was thinking of her or her dignified exit.

'What about Tom?' Jeremy demanded.

'Oh!' Cressida cried guiltily. 'Oh, how awful! I've forgotten to read Tom's letter. And I've had it ever since yesterday morning.'

Jeremy began to smile, his brow lifting towards his hairline.

'Must you now?'

'Oh, yes, I must. It's so rude not to. Poor Tom. He'll think I don't care.'

235

'And do you?'

Cressida frowned perplexedly. 'Jeremy! Please don't confuse me. I—I don't know. We don't like the same things. I—I ran away from that awful bed. It had a headboard like a tombstone. Let me at least read his letter.'

She took it from the mantelpiece and tore it open. Jeremy began to fidget about the room. He did not for one moment intend to let her forget his presence. Mimosa came in and began to cry for attention, his tail fluffed, his golden eyes all guile. Jeremy swung him into his arms, and listened for the deep appreciative purr.

'Shall we go to Paris? Shall we leave unresponsive girls with dull fiancés in the country to look after themselves?'

'Oh!' cried Cressida. 'Oh! The wretch! Why, he can't be faithful even for a week. Oh, I'd never have believed it!'

Jeremy snatched the letter from her. He read, '*I can't help feeling, Cress, that I am going to grow very fond of Mary Madden. She and I have a great deal in common—*'

Jeremy tossed the letter into the air and gave a great shout of laughter.

'Good old Tom! Salt of the earth Tom!'

'Jeremy, you don't care a bit that I'm slighted!'

'Slighted, did you say?' He had her in his arms and was kissing her in a way she had never been kissed before. 'Is this slighting you? Or this? Oh, Cressida Lucy, I've adored you ever since you tumbled down Arabia's front steps practically into my arms. Don't you love me, too? Don't you give me all that love you've never given Tom? Cressida, listen to me! I'm asking you a question.'

She did love him, of course. She had known she was going to fall in love with him from the moment she had opened her eyes that day and seen his bright gaze on her. And what was more, everyone else had known, even gentle Mr. Mullins who had been so perturbed about her friendship with Arabia because of Arabia's tragic history, but whose loyalty had forbidden him to speak of it.

Jeremy, however, was altogether too confident. He deserved to go through a little suspense. She did not mean to answer him for a little. But all at once she had a thought, a joke to share, and she could not prevent her face dimpling with happiness that here was someone with whom to share jokes all her life.

'Jeremy!' she said naughtily. 'Let's send Tom a Victorian what-not for a wedding present. He'll adore it!'

A